GAP
LIFE

GAP LIFE

JOHN COY

FEIWEL AND FRIENDS
NEW YORK

A Feiwel and Friends Book
An imprint of Macmillan Publishing Group, LLC

Gap Life. Copyright © 2016 by John Coy. All rights reserved.
Printed in the United States of America by R. R. Donnelley & Sons Company,
Harrisonburg, Virginia. For information, address Feiwel and Friends,
175 Fifth Avenue, New York, N.Y. 10010.

Our books may be purchased in bulk for promotional, educational, or
business use. Please contact your local bookseller or the Macmillan Corporate
and Premium Sales Department at (800) 221-7945 ext. 5442 or by e-mail at
MacmillanSpecialMarkets@macmillan.com.

Library of Congress Control Number: 2016937596

ISBN 978-1-250-08895-6 (hardcover) / ISBN 978-1-250-08896-3 (ebook)

Book design by Anna Booth
Feiwel and Friends logo designed by Filomena Tuosto

First Edition—2016

10 9 8 7 6 5 4 3 2 1

fiercereads.com

for F

THE END

THE END. It was really the end. My right heel tapped away as I sat among three hundred Clairemont High School graduates and watched Nora Engdahl, our valedictorian, stride confidently to the podium. Nora, who'd never gotten a B in her life and was headed to Stanford, paused and brushed back her straight blond hair as she looked around the gym.

"She's hot." Garret Frampton, who'd started drinking early, announced the obvious.

"Definitely." I rubbed the sleeve of my shiny blue robe.

"Party out at the Land tonight," Frampton said. "Be there."

I half listened to Nora tell us that graduation was only the beginning and that we were all embarking on the great adventure of our lives, but that wasn't how I was feeling.

High school graduation was the end. Unlike my friends, who were excited about their fall plans, I was carrying a secret. And as Nora continued on about pursuing our passions and creating a brighter future, that secret weighed on me, heavier than ever.

———————

LATER THAT NIGHT, after pictures, congratulations, and parental warnings to be safe, Jett Morrison and I ran down the path through the woods on Frampton's dad's land.

"We're free!" Jett hollered as he approached the crowd gathered around the keg in the clearing.

I chased after him but didn't feel free.

Frampton handed me a red plastic cup of beer and took a drink from his tequila bottle. "Lockermates for seven years." Frampton banged his bottle against my cup and beer sloshed out.

"Yeah," I said, trying to get into the spirit of the warm summer night.

"Going to miss you, dude." Frampton stretched out his arm for a half hug. I slid over to avoid spilling more beer as Jett moved over by the big rocks to talk to Nora and her friend Teagan Kleist.

"I had to work so hard to get into Madison." Frampton hit me with a blast of tequila breath. "Now I'll party all freshman year."

I stepped back and tripped on a root. College was the last thing I wanted to talk about.

"I'll be paying off student loans forever, so I'm gonna get my money's worth." Frampton took another drink. "Madtown gets wild."

I took a sip of beer. "Hey, Framp, I gotta talk to Jett."

"Party 'til it's light." He lifted his bottle as I walked away.

"Yeah." After talking to Frampton every school day since sixth grade, I didn't know when I'd see him again.

"Congratulations, Cray!" Kenna Laughlin waved. I'd gone out with her a couple of times at the start of the year without it turning into anything.

"You too." She was one of those girls who was friends with everybody—that was why she was class president—and she was smart. She'd applied to about twenty different colleges, gotten accepted at most of them, and chose Cornell after they gave her a ton of money.

"So you're all set for premed at St. Luke's."

"Not quite." I hugged her and moved toward Jett as moonlight filtered through the pines.

"Nice speech, Nora." I raised my cup and she lifted hers in a toast.

"It wasn't that great." She adjusted her bra strap as Jett watched. She was a star volleyballer and Jett had been after her all year.

"Can you believe we're finished?" Teagan shook her blond bangs and held a big smile. "Make sure you all come to my graduation party Saturday. We'll have tons of food."

I took a gulp of beer. Mom had been all over me about making plans for my party.

"We did it." Jett high-fived everybody. He didn't drink, because he had a basketball scholarship to Duluth. He was the first in his family to go to college, and he followed training rules year-round.

"And we're all off to different schools in the fall." Nora grinned like she couldn't wait to start.

I didn't have the guts to tell the truth. I turned away to watch some theater girls down by the creek singing the school song. I couldn't keep my secret much longer, but I wasn't ready to deal with it, so I tried to lose myself in the party.

After that, everything blurred together. Jett left with Nora and didn't come back. There were bonfires, beer, and vodka shots. People paired off and disappeared into the woods. Others got totally smashed and hugged one another, promising to stay connected forever. I did my best to pretend I was into it, but my fear of telling my parents about my decision tugged at me.

TEAGAN DROVE ME BACK AFTER THE ALL-NIGHT PARTY, her pink fingernails flashing against the steering wheel as the sun rose above the trees. "I've been accepted at Beloit, but I'm on the waiting list at Carleton." Teagan talked fast. "My aunt went to Carleton and really wants me to go there, but my parents say I should let it go and focus on Beloit, but I can't. Carleton's a better school and I love Northfield, but if Carleton says yes, I don't know if they'll give me the same financial aid. I feel trapped in between. The whole process is crazy."

I tried to listen but was colleged out. I wanted a different topic, anything else.

"What do you think I should do, Cray?"

"Me? I don't know. What do you want to do?"

"Go to Carleton. But they don't want me. I did everything I was supposed to do: got involved in clubs, stuck with gymnastics even after I tore ligaments, did well on my tests, got good grades, and wrote an interesting essay, and I still didn't get in."

She looked at me expectantly, but I was the last person to offer advice.

"I feel like a failure," she said.

"You're not a failure, Teagan. You'll do fine wherever you go."

"Thanks, Cray."

I asked her to drop me off at the gas station by the university since it was too early to go home without risking running into Dad.

When she stopped the car, she beckoned me with her pink-tipped finger, like she had something to whisper. I unbuckled my seat belt and leaned in. She grabbed the back of my head and pulled my face to hers. Teagan's hair smelled of cigarettes and beer, but her breath was cinnamony fresh as our lips met. Her tongue darted around my mouth as I shifted my position to get a better angle. She kept her eyes closed, so I did, too, and her lips pressed harder against mine.

Just then a car pulled into the spot next to us and Teagan straightened up. I watched the old guy who'd interrupted us take forever to turn off his engine and open his door. He stuck a wooden cane out the door and it took even longer for him to stand, the slowest guy getting out of a car in history.

I turned to Teagan, who was adjusting her bangs in the rear-view mirror, and wondered if we'd go back to what we were doing, but she acted like she'd already moved on.

"I've got to go, Cray," she said breezily, as if the kiss hadn't even happened.

"Thanks for the ride." I opened my door.

"Happy graduation," she called.

"Yeah, you too."

I wandered the empty aisles of the store thinking about the kiss. My breath probably tasted like a mix of beer, pizza, and Doritos. No wonder Teagan wanted to stop kissing. I bought three glazed doughnuts and two packs of gum. My head throbbed from the beer, the bright fluorescent lights, and being up all night, but I couldn't go home. Dad would still be getting ready for work.

I devoured the doughnuts as I walked across campus. I stopped at a water fountain for a long drink. My first day with no school felt kind of empty as I wandered down to the river and popped gum into my mouth. I stood at the edge and watched water splash against rocks and lost myself in a trance. After a while, I climbed the steps to the dirt path that curved downstream.

At a bench, I sat and listened to birds chatter away before

humans got up to claim the day. Exhaustion pulled me down as I checked the time on my phone.

Even though I didn't want to, I had to get it over with. I had to tell my parents. But first, I desperately needed some sleep.

I headed home, hoping it was safe to do so.

NO DEAL

ALL I WANTED TO DO WAS CRASH. I walked up the flower-lined driveway to our big house and quietly opened the back door. I kicked off my shoes in the entryway and smelled coffee and French toast as my mom talked with my eighth-grade brother, Lansing. I went into the kitchen to let them know I was home before going straight to bed.

"Where the hell have you been?" Dad glared at me from the table.

"Uh…um…a graduation party. I told Mom." I'd thought for sure he'd be gone.

"You didn't tell me."

I jammed my hands into my pockets and felt more like a kinder-gartner than a high school graduate. Lansing, who was a math and science wizard, glanced up and then poured maple syrup on his French toast.

"Thank God you're finally home." Mom adjusted the clip in her hair. "We didn't give you a curfew, but I certainly expected you back before now. You didn't answer any of my texts."

"Sorry, my phone died."

"Have you been drinking?" She examined me like a science experiment gone wrong. "Your eyes are bloodshot."

"I'm just tired." I was glad I'd chewed the gum to hide the smell.

"You're only seventeen," Dad declared.

"I'm almost eighteen."

"Either way. You're underage and living here. We're not having you crawl home at all hours after you've been out drinking."

I'd had less to drink than most people, but I knew there was no point in arguing with him. That just made things worse. "I'm going to bed."

"Not so fast." Dad stood up. "You and I need to talk."

Lansing smirked, and I could have smacked him. I followed Dad into the living room and imagined putting on a suit of armor to protect myself from another one of his lectures. He pointed to the brown leather couch, and I sat down.

"Let's get one thing straight. High school's over. It's time to start acting like an adult." Dad towered over me as I looked past him at his two treasured blue-and-white Chinese vases protected in their secure glass cases. He didn't like to travel, but he loved collecting things that he thought would increase in value.

I rubbed my eyes. "How come you're not at work?"

"For your information, I didn't have surgeries this morning. I went up to your room and you weren't there, so I've been sitting here listening to your mother worry."

"Sorry." I looked down at the orange-and-brown carpet, Dad's favorite, which had been handmade in Pakistan.

"In the fall, we're not going to be around to remind you of everything. You'll need to be responsible for getting your work done and keeping your grades up so you can get into a top medical school."

I stared at the complex carpet pattern. Dad had talked about me being a doctor since I was little, and last fall, he'd made me apply early decision to St. Luke's, where he and his dad had gone. When I was accepted, he made it clear that he'd pay for everything as long as I studied premed.

"College will be much more demanding," he continued. "You can't coast like you did in high school."

I hadn't coasted. I'd worked hard but hadn't met his standard of straight As. I looked up at him in his jacket and tie and thought about my decision.

"You have to concentrate in every class, every lab from day one. You have to prove you have what it takes to be a doctor."

Three glazed doughnuts on top of beer, pizza, and Doritos churned in my stomach. My head felt like it was about to explode as he droned on. Finally, I couldn't take the pressure anymore.

I blurted it out before I could stop. "I'm not going to be a doctor."

"What?" Dad's face tightened.

"I'm not going to be a doctor."

Dad stared down at me. "Yes you are. You're Crayton Robert Franklin, the third. Your grandfather was a doctor. I'm a doctor. I expect you to carry on the tradition."

Doctor. I hated that word.

"Your uncle Ed's a doctor," Dad continued. "Your cousins are preparing to be doctors, and Ed doesn't miss an opportunity to tell me how well they're doing."

"Jacob's not going to be one." I rubbed my hands on my pants.

"He doesn't count," Dad shot back.

"Why not?"

"He's got special needs. He can't be a doctor."

"He still counts."

"Of course he counts." Spit flew out of Dad's mouth.

The back door closed as Lansing left to catch his bus for his last day of middle school. Mom turned on the super-quiet new dishwasher and it hummed.

"There are plenty of specialties to choose from," Dad said. "Oncology, radiology, anesthesiology. I know that, like your mother, you're not great around blood, but many areas of medicine don't require that."

He didn't need to bring up my fainting, which hadn't happened in a long time. "I want to take classes I'm interested in, like Spanish, history, and English. I'm not even that good in math and science."

"That's because you don't work hard. If you did, you'd do fine." Dad sat down in his leather chair and grabbed the arms. "You've been accepted at St. Luke's. We've paid the deposit. Everything's set."

I shook my head. St. Luke's was a small, all-male Catholic college out in the middle of nowhere. I'd never wanted to go to an all-guys school, but Dad had determined that was the only place I should apply.

"I decided I'm not going."

"*You* decided?" Dad shot out of his chair and got in my face. "Are you crazy?"

Mom rushed into the living room. "What on earth is happening?"

"Tell her." Dad's face was pinched with anger.

"I'm not going to St. Luke's. I don't want to be a doctor." I tried to say it confidently, since it was the biggest decision I'd made in my life. "I know you want me to, but I can't."

Mom looked from me to Dad and then back. "What do you want, then?"

"I don't know. I'm good in Spanish. Maybe I could be a translator and travel to different countries—"

"A translator?" Dad cut me off. "Who's hiring you for that?"

"We're offering to pay all that money." Mom paced next to the grand piano.

"You could graduate from college and med school debt-free." Dad's face was getting redder. "Who gets that kind of opportunity these days?"

Mom looked like she was about to cry. "How can you be so ungrateful, Cray?"

"I'm not ungrateful, but I can't do it this way."

Dad shook his head like I disgusted him. "You're making a monumental mistake."

"And we're in the middle of planning your graduation party." Mom paced faster.

"If you don't get your act together, we're not having any damn party," Dad said. "I don't want a houseful of people hearing you're not going to St. Luke's."

I sank deeper into the couch. "So what happens if I don't accept your deal?"

"You'll accept it." Dad leaned over and banged his fist on the table, and the lamp shook.

I started to stand up.

"Sit down!" he yelled. "What do you plan to do?"

"I don't know," I said quietly.

"You need to figure it out, fast." He jabbed a finger at me.

Like I could solve this after being out all night.

"You can start by getting a job. You've had it way too easy around here. The free ride is over," Dad shouted. "While you're pretending to be unsure about St. Luke's, you'll pay rent to get a taste of what not being in college is really like."

"Crayton," Mom pleaded, turning to Dad. "Isn't there some way to fix this?"

"He needs to learn to accept consequences, Miriam. He's not a little boy anymore."

"I'm late for work." Mom pulled a tissue from her pocket and held it in the air like she'd forgotten what to do with it. She wiped her eyes, crumpled it up, and shoved it back in her pocket. "We'll work this out later. You're going to St. Luke's. That's what we've planned. We'll talk about it at dinner."

I heard the door close and listened as she started her Audi to go off to her dietician job at the hospital.

"We're not standing by while you make a selfish damn decision." Now Dad was pacing. "Selfish, immature, cowardly. You'd ruin your future. You'd regret it every single day of your life."

I wasn't listening, just waiting for him to stop as my head pounded. I felt like I'd floated up to the ceiling and was watching everything from there.

"When I get home this afternoon, you need to have a job. Understand?"

I nodded.

"Say it out loud. Do you understand?"

"Yes." I bowed my head and squeezed my hands together as he went on about my selfishness. Maybe I was making a monumental mistake. But I'd be miserable if I went to St. Luke's and he chose my classes and what I'd become. That would be an even bigger mistake.

AFTER DOWNING A COUPLE OF ADVIL, I closed the shades in my room and got into bed. My brain was bursting, but I wasn't doing anything until I got some sleep. I charged my phone and set the alarm for three so I'd be gone before any of them got home.

I lay back and tried to push thoughts of Dad out of my mind. *Selfish*. He was the one being selfish by picking St. Luke's and insisting I be a doctor. Of course I should have acted sooner, back when he had me apply to only one college, but I wasn't ready then.

What are you going to do? What do you want to be? Everyone was asking the same questions, and I was sick of it and didn't have answers.

There was one thing, though, that I was one hundred percent sure about. I knew what I didn't want to be. I didn't want to be anything like my dad.

RAYNE MAN

I MADE SURE I WAS OUT OF THE HOUSE before anyone else returned. My head still hurt as I walked downtown and replayed what had happened. Holy shit. Instead of going to college like my friends, I was looking for a job to pay rent at home. I'd thrown it all away, and for what?

Division Street, the center of downtown, was quiet as I crossed to Sam's Pizza. "Do you have job applications?" I asked the woman at the counter as I inhaled the smell of melted cheese.

"Yep, they're here somewhere." She had gray streaks in her dark hair, which was pulled back with a red headband. "You can fill out one of these, but to be honest, we're not hiring. Don't get your hopes up."

"It's not worth it?"

"Go ahead; you never know when someone will split or end up in the psych ward." She pushed me a pen. "It's hot out there. What do you like to drink?"

"Sprite, thanks."

She filled a plastic cup with ice while I started on the application.

For employment history I listed last summer's job bussing tables at the country club. Dad had made me do that to "learn the value of hard work," and the place was full of his doctor friends who'd ask me about college. I definitely wasn't going back there.

I went through the questions and paused when I came to *Why do you want to work at Sam's?* I couldn't write the truth about Dad, so I wrote that Sam's had the best pizza in the world.

I sat back and slurped my Sprite. That answer wasn't too bad.

The woman looked over my application and smiled. "I'm Sam. I'll call if anything opens up."

THE MARQUEE OF BUDGET CINEMA STUCK OUT OVER the sidewalk. I could collect tickets and put popcorn in tubs. I opened the door and felt the coolness. AC would be a plus. The person at the ticket booth wore a white short-sleeved shirt and a black bow tie, which was a definite drawback.

"Hey, who do I talk to about applying for a job?"

"Didn't you just graduate?" The kid's braces flashed.

"Yeah."

"My sister did, too."

Big deal, I thought, but then remembered. "You're Teagan's brother, right?"

"Yep." He adjusted his bow tie. "They usually hire younger kids."

"So it's not worth applying."

"Not really." He shrugged like he was sympathetic.

"Where's Teagan working this summer?"

"Lifeguarding at Lake Winona. Working on her tan."

"Tell her hi from Cray."

Zero for two. I thought about where friends were working. Some guys from the basketball team were counselors at a camp up by the Boundary Waters, but those jobs had been set up months ago. I walked past the post office. I could sort mail, even deliver it, but they didn't hire people off the street. You probably had to take some kind of test, and they didn't hire high school kids. But I wasn't a high school kid anymore. I was a graduate. I was in between— too old for high school jobs, too young for adult jobs.

Then I realized I wasn't looking for a summer job. I was looking for a real job. I couldn't afford to pay for college on my own. Maybe if I held my ground for a year, my parents would give in and pay for me to go where I wanted. Maybe not. Whatever job I got might not be temporary. It could be my JOB for a long time.

Oh, God, that was too depressing to think about.

I kept hoping I'd see a sign: HELP WANTED, RECENT HIGH SCHOOL GRADUATE, EXCELLENT PAY! That wasn't happening. There weren't many people walking around downtown on a Wednesday afternoon. That was part of the problem. Downtown Clairemont was dead.

If I wanted a job, I'd have to search online or go out to the mall, where more businesses were. I called Jett.

He picked up after the first ring. "Cray Man, what are you doing?"

"Looking for a job." I kicked an empty Red Bull can into the street. "You want to run out to the mall?"

"Yeah, Nora's scooping ice cream at Malley's. I'll shower and pick you up."

"Not at my house. Meet me at the Edge Coffee Shop on Front Street." I shoved my phone in my pocket. Jett had no idea that the reason I needed a job was because I wasn't going to college. A tidal wave of panic smashed against me. Maybe Dad was right. Maybe at seventeen, I was ruining my life.

THE EDGE WAS A STATE UNIVERSITY HANGOUT WHERE people looked at their laptops and studied. I ordered an iced coffee from a guy with bushy sideburns. "Do you have any job openings?"

"Any experience working in a coffee shop?"

"No."

"Then you wouldn't have a chance." He filled a cup with ice.

"If you can't get a job without experience, how do you get experience in the first place?"

"One of life's mysteries." He poured my iced coffee. "You've got to find someone who'll give you a break."

"And they don't do that here?"

"No, they require a year of coffee shop experience."

I pulled bills out of my wallet. Nothing was working.

"Try Starbucks at the mall." He handed me my change. "They hire without experience."

"Thanks." I dropped the coins into the tip jar. I wasn't sure about applying at Starbucks. Making all those different drinks exactly the way people wanted seemed complicated.

I sat down in a cushy chair in the corner and sipped my coffee. Fortunately, I still had some money in savings that Grandpa Franklin had left me when he died. But it wasn't close to enough to pay for college on my own. I desperately needed someone to hire me.

I scrolled through job sites on my phone but everything required experience. I didn't have a car to get to the places that were farther away, either.

Across the room a girl with brown chopped-off hair sat by the window writing in a journal. Her hair stuck out at odd angles like she'd cut it with a Weedwacker. She wore red Chucks, tight army shorts, and a lime-green tank top without a bra. She stopped writing, put her pen in her mouth, and looked over at me.

I turned away quickly. When she started writing again, I resumed watching. She turned the page and her pen flew across the paper.

"Cray Man." Jett came through the door. "Ready?"

"Yeah." I stood and finished my coffee.

Jett turned toward the journal girl. "Hey, Rayne."

"Jettster." She closed her journal.

"You two know each other?" Jett pointed to me.

She smiled. "I don't think so." Despite her weird hair and odd clothes, she was pretty, even as she tried to hide it.

"Rayne, Cray."

"Hey," I said.

"I remember you." She had large brown eyes with long, dark lashes. "We rode the same bus in sixth grade and you boys used to sit in back and make fun of the driver. You called him Captain Crunch and imitated his deep voice."

"Wow, you've got a great memory." I tried to hold her gaze, but that tank top made it hard.

"Rayne remembers everything," Jett said.

She shook her head. "Some things I try to forget."

I stared at her. Her shy smile, that wild hair, her no-bra boldness. Who was she?

I CLIMBED INTO JETT'S OLD PICKUP. I wasn't going to college and didn't have a job, but I felt better. "How come I never saw Rayne around school?"

"She's into art and took most of her classes at the university this year. She's different." Jett started the truck. "She never came to games or dances."

"Why not?" I buckled my seat belt.

"Not into it."

"She smart?"

"Super smart." Jett looked over his shoulder and pulled out. "She saved me in English when I first moved here. I'd never had to work at my old school because teachers passed the jocks through. I asked Rayne for help because I sat next to her and she knew everything. I got an A in that class, and after that, teachers started treating me like I was smart."

"Where's she going to college?"

"I don't think she's going."

"Why not?"

"I don't know. You'll have to ask her."

"Where's she live?"

"Someplace downtown, I think."

I couldn't remember my sixth-grade bus route, and I certainly didn't remember anybody like her.

"You're asking a lot of questions." Jett looked over at me. "Slow down, Rayne Man."

I couldn't. I kept thinking of her in that lime-green top.

HELP WANTED

I WENT UP AND DOWN THE MALL SEARCHING FOR HELP WANTED or POSITION AVAILABLE signs but didn't find any.

Maybe I was too late. I should have started a month ago, but back then I didn't know I was going to have to pay rent to live at home. At the bookstore, a woman with purple-framed glasses stared at a screen while a guy with dreadlocks stacked books. I could do that.

I cleared my throat. "I'm interested in applying for a job."

"Go to our website," the woman said without looking up.

"Are there any positions available?"

"No."

The story was the same at the copy shop, the department store, the arcade, and the frozen yogurt stand. A couple of places gave me paper applications even though they didn't have openings. I sat down at an orange table in the food court and filled them out, but even as I did, I knew it was useless. Nobody was going to look at them.

My head throbbed. I was so desperate that I went outside and crossed the street to a place I never dreamed I'd apply: McDonald's.

"Hi, I'm interested in working here," I said to a guy whose name tag read JAVON.

"I'll get the manager."

I focused on his teal-and-purple uniform. I'd hate wearing that, but I could deal with it until I got something better.

The manager, whose name tag read KEITH, marched up to the counter. He was about thirty and looked irritated, like I'd interrupted something important.

"You want to work here?" He had a buzz cut and a thin mustache.

"Yes, I'd like to apply."

"Why do you want to work at McDonald's?"

"Because I need a job." His lips turned down, and I knew I'd answered wrong. "Because I think it's a…" I couldn't say what I really thought—that it was a place to work if you couldn't get anything else. "Good place to eat," I finished lamely. "It's fast and convenient."

He frowned like he was sucking on a piece of bitter fruit. "What kind of experience do you have in the food-service industry?"

The food-service industry! He acted like I wanted to run a McDonald's, not wear a goofy uniform and put baskets of fries in hot oil.

"I have experience bussing tables at the country club."

"Fill out an application online or grab one of those green forms." He pointed to a display by the beverage station.

"You don't have any openings now?"

"No." He turned his back on me.

I picked up an application and sat at a table in front of a grinning Ronald McDonald. I started filling it out and got stuck on how I heard about "this employment opportunity." I crumpled the paper and threw it in the trash. I couldn't even get a job at McDonald's.

Ronald McDonald kept grinning at me, so I gave him the finger and walked out.

"ANYBODY HIRE YOU?" Jett asked when I returned to Malley's.

"Nope."

"They don't have openings here, but I could check at the law firm where I'm interning," Nora said. She leaned over and wiped around the ice-cream tubs while Jett and I admired the number of buttons she'd left undone. "What kind of work are you interested in?"

"Anything. I need something right away, but I'd prefer not to wear a stupid uniform."

She lifted her leg to show a blue stripe on her khaki shorts. "Like this."

"No, that's not bad."

"A little lame," Jett teased. "But you look great."

Nora smiled as she packed napkins into a holder.

"You want to get some pizza?" Jett turned to me.

"Yeah, I'm starving."

"Trust me, the pizza at the food court is terrible." Nora made a face.

"Let's run down to Sam's," Jett said. "How late do you work, Nora?"

"Until closing. Nine."

"We'll come back and pick you up."

"Thanks." Nora winked at him, so smoothly it didn't even seem planned.

JETT AND I SLID INTO OUR FAVORITE BOOTH, but I didn't see Sam anywhere. Jett was solidly built and a magnet for girls, and I was a tall, skinny virgin with big ears and a scar running from the corner of my eye toward my ear from an accident with a slide. We made an odd pair, but we'd been best friends since freshman year. I'd helped Jett adjust to a new school and we stayed tight even when he became a basketball star and I sat at the end of the bench.

"Large, extra cheese?" Jett asked.

"Yeah." We didn't need to look at the menu.

The server, probably a university student, pulled out her pad but didn't have a pen and left to find one. Maybe she was one of the employees who would quit. That might be the only way I'd get a job.

The server came back and took our order. She wrote slowly and at the end added, "Two Cokes."

"No, one Coke, one Sprite." I could do this job better than she did.

Jett texted away on his phone. People always wanted to do stuff with him. I checked mine: nothing interesting. The waitress brought our drinks and two straws, but she set the Coke in front of me. I passed it to Jett and grabbed the Sprite so she'd see her mistake.

"I've got to get a job." I unwrapped my straw. "My dad's making me pay rent."

"Why?"

I told him about Dad not paying for college unless I studied premed at St. Luke's. And about deciding not to go.

Jett's jaw dropped open. "What the hell, Cray? When were you going to tell me? That's major-league crazy."

"What I'm doing or what he's doing?"

"Both. Can't you go and study what you want?"

"No, my dad knows everybody up there. He'd choose my classes and keep track of everything." I watched the waitress mix up another order.

"Can't you apply somewhere else?"

"They wouldn't pay for it, and there's no way I'd qualify for financial aid with their income. I can't afford college on my own."

Jett slurped his Coke. "You can't just take the money and run?"

"You know my dad. He controls everything. He's not about to give me money and let me decide." I slouched down in the booth. "Don't tell anybody. I'm not ready to deal with it."

"Okay. If I didn't have a full ride to Duluth, my folks couldn't afford college, but yours can. That's so messed up. You should be going. What will you do?"

"I don't know. Right now, I can't go home without a job."

"You can stay at my house." Jett held up his glass for a refill. "My folks are always cool with you staying over."

"Thanks." I texted Lansing to tell Mom and Dad since I didn't want to get into it with them.

"I wish I knew someplace you could work," Jett said.

Lansing texted back: *r u really not going to St. L? Insane!*

Just tell em. I turned off my phone. I didn't want to talk to anybody in my family.

WHEN JETT AND I WALKED OUT, music was blaring from the courthouse square. A Brazilian band was playing, and the lead singer pleaded with people to dance. Most of the audience, which was mainly families with children and old people who'd brought their own camping chairs, declined.

The only people dancing were three little kids and a chubby guy with Down syndrome. He reminded me of my cousin Jacob as he bopped back and forth and didn't care what anybody thought.

"Good dancing, Sean," the woman beside us shouted. She had big glasses and sat next to two other people eating ice-cream bars.

The band jammed away despite the lack of dancers. I scanned the crowd but didn't see anybody I knew. By the corner, a woman waited for customers at an ice-cream cart. I could do that, but business was slow so she probably wasn't hiring somebody new.

In front of us, a couple of guys about Lansing's age laughed.

"He looks like a robot." The skinny one pointed at the man dancing.

"More like a retard," the heavier one said.

I pushed him in the back.

"Hey, what are you doing?" He turned around.

"Watch your mouth."

The heavier one looked like he was about to say something but then saw Jett.

"Let's get ice cream." His friend pulled him away.

"Like that guy should talk," Jett said.

I thought about Jacob and how often he heard stupid stuff from people who were supposed to be smarter than he was. So many of them forgot that we all have our handicaps.

BACK AT JETT'S, we played *Call of Duty* and polished off a bag of Twix. His folks and younger sisters stayed upstairs, and Jett had the finished basement for his bedroom and an entertainment room with a mini fridge that his mom kept stocked. His house was a lot smaller than ours, but more comfortable, and his folks left us alone. At a quarter to nine, we went to get Nora.

As we waited, I thought about how hard it would be to work at the mall. I wouldn't be able to borrow Mom's car all the time, and it was a long way to bike. The bus would take forever. I needed something downtown, something closer to home.

Nora came out of Malley's and Jett flipped her bike into the back of the truck. The three of us squished together in front, with Nora, who smelled like ice cream and perfume, in the middle.

Jett talked about basketball camp and Nora described how she liked working at the law office and seeing what it took to be a lawyer. I looked out the window at all the stores where other people worked. Jett had his job. Nora had two. They both were headed to college and now they had each other.

I didn't have shit.

LUCKY DAY

THE NEXT MORNING I WOKE UP ON JETT'S COUCH and couldn't fall back to sleep. I shifted around but kept thinking about how screwed up not going to college was, like a bad dream with no end.

I got up, dressed, and left quietly for the Edge. I walked the ten blocks hoping Rayne would be there, but when I arrived, she wasn't. Instead a parade of businesspeople lined up for their daily fix and hurried off. I poured sugar into my cappuccino and checked out Instagram. I texted Jett thanks for letting me stay over and played Solitaire on my phone. I lost every time.

And when I looked up, Rayne was sitting at her table, writing. How had she appeared without my noticing? She was wearing baggy jean shorts and a tight orange T-shirt with a broken peace sign down the middle. Disappointingly, she had a bra on underneath.

She turned and met my gaze. "What are you looking at, Cray?"

"Umm, nothing. I mean, your shirt." I picked up my phone and coffee and went over.

"They're just boobs," she said. "Women have 'em, you know."

"What are you writing?" I couldn't believe she'd said that.

"Not writing. Drawing." She closed her book.

"Can I see?"

"Sure." She slid it over and opened the page.

Looking straight up at me was me. The drawing had my scar and short hair and big ears. The mouth was right. The eyes were right. But what surprised me was the expression—a certain sadness I didn't realize anybody else saw.

"Wow, you're good."

"I hope it's okay." She ran her hand through her wild hair.

"Okay? Are you kidding? It's great."

"No, I mean that I was drawing you without your permission."

"That's fine." I peered at the drawing. It was like she saw inside of me.

"How did you get your scar?" she asked.

"When I was eight, I was chasing my cousin and tripped and hit my face on the corner of a slide and cut it open pretty bad. Dad rushed me to the clinic and stitched me up himself."

"Your dad's a doc?"

"Yeah, a cardiovascular surgeon."

"That's close to your eye. You were lucky."

"I know."

"Everybody's got scars," Rayne said. "Some show more than others."

I nodded. This girl was definitely different. "Can I get you a coffee?"

"I don't drink coffee, but I'd love a green tea."

The espresso machine whirred while I waited at the counter

and Rayne resumed drawing. I ordered a large green tea and pointed to a blueberry-walnut scone. "One of those, please."

I returned to the table. "For you."

"That's sweet, but I don't eat wheat."

"Why not?" I glanced at her shirt again and tried to guess what a broken peace sign meant.

"I'm allergic. I get bad headaches from wheat." She blew on her tea and took a sip.

"So you don't eat bread or muffins or scones?"

"Only if they're wheat-free. Three days a week they have wheat-free muffins here."

I broke off a corner of the scone and ate it. "I can't imagine not eating wheat. I love it."

"I do, too." She smiled. "Sometimes what we love isn't good for us."

I stared at her. She had clear natural skin. No makeup as far as I could tell.

"Not eating wheat doesn't make me love it less," she said. "I probably love it more than you since you can eat it whenever you want. We're human—we love what we can't have."

I felt guilty about eating when she couldn't. "Do they have anything that doesn't have wheat today?"

"Only chocolate-covered macaroons."

"Can I get you one?"

"No, thanks. I've got this." She pulled a banana out of her backpack and peeled it. "Would you like a bite?" She held out the banana.

"No, I'm good." It felt a bit weird.

"Sure?"

What the hell—it was just a banana. I bit off the end and we both laughed.

I picked a walnut off the scone and brushed crumbs off it. "Walnut?"

She stuck it on the top of her banana and bit it in a sexy way. "Mmmmm."

Wow. Rayne wasn't like Teagan or Kenna or any other girls I knew. "What are you doing this summer?"

"Making money for my gap year." She wiped her mouth.

"What's that?" I broke off another chunk of scone.

"I'm taking time to travel. I want to see the world and experience new things."

"And you'll still go to college?"

"Yeah, at some point, but I'm in no hurry. The application process encourages dishonesty, and I'm glad to have a break." She rolled the banana peel into a ball. "Last fall, one of the counselors told us to be sure to apply to a safety school. A safety school? Should we pick a safety career? A safety life? Who wants to live like that?" She shrugged and opened her arms. "So many people act like where they're accepted determines their future. They've got way more control over their lives than that."

I nodded. I hadn't thought about any of this. All I knew was that I didn't want to be a doctor. I didn't know what came next.

"Besides, living abroad will make me more interesting to colleges when I do apply. It's not why I'm going, but I get the game." Rayne wrapped the banana peel in a napkin.

"Where are you traveling?"

"Scotland to start. I've got a thing for bagpipes and guys in kilts, and my grandfather, who was Scottish, taught me 'Over the Sea to

Skye' when I was little." She leaned in and started singing, as if singing in a coffee shop was no big deal.

Speed, bonnie boat, like a bird on the wing,
Onward! the sailors cry;
Carry the lord that's born to be King
Over the sea to Skye.

Rayne looked at me as she sang, and I suddenly felt like every girl I'd ever known had been practice for meeting her.

Loud the winds howl, loud the waves roar,
Thunderclaps rend the air;
Baffled, our foes stand by the shore,
Follow they will not dare.

The song was mysterious and I wanted more. I could have stared at her and listened for hours.

"So I'm working to save money to get to Skye."

"Where do you work?"

"Two places. One's in the art department at the university, and the other's a place called Oakcrest where four adults who have disabilities live. They all have jobs during the day, and I sleep over four nights a week."

"You get paid to sleep?" I finished off my cappuccino.

"Exactly," she said. "I go in at ten and leave at seven when the morning person comes in. I'm there in case of an emergency. What about you? What are you doing this summer?"

"Looking for work. I need a job." My heel tapped away as I talked.

"What kind of job?" She swirled the tea in her cup.

"Anything that pays."

"Today might be your lucky day, my friend."

"I could use some luck."

"Rebecca, the woman who works opposite me on Thursday, Friday, and Saturday nights, is having hip surgery," Rayne said. "Everybody loves her, but she's out for the summer and we need someone to cover three nights a week. I can't because they don't like paying overtime."

"I'm good at sleeping. I've had lots of practice." Finally something I was qualified for.

"Do you have any experience with people with developmental disabilities?"

"Yeah, my cousin Jacob, the one I was chasing when I cut my face, has Down syndrome. We're the same age and always hang out at family events."

"Good." Rayne finished her tea.

I thought about anything else that would help. "I shut up a couple of guys last night who used the word *retard*."

Rayne nodded. "Ever been convicted of a sex crime?"

"No," I said quickly.

"I didn't think so." She laughed.

"Why are you helping me like this?" As soon as I said it, I knew I sounded suspicious.

"I like your vibe, and helping people is good karma. Besides, I think you'd be a good fit." Rayne stood up.

I was glad to see she was tall. Not as tall as I was, but at least five foot ten. Tall was good.

"Let's go see about getting you that job."

EXPERIENCE

I FOLLOWED RAYNE DOWN THE HALL OF THE THIRD floor of an old building, a place I never would have looked for a job. She pushed open a door marked CLAIREMONT SUPPORT SERVICES and held it for me.

"Rayne." A large woman greeted her.

"Lydia, this is my friend Cray." She turned to me. "Lydia's the office manager. She's the one who really runs things around here."

Lydia smiled. "What brings you in so early?"

"Cray's a possibility to sub for Rebecca."

I shifted my feet while Lydia looked me over. "Do you have experience with adults with developmental disabilities?"

Experience. Experience. Experience. It seemed impossible to get started if you didn't have experience.

"Yes," Rayne said. "His cousin has Down syndrome." She looked at me to see what I'd add.

"Yeah, my cousin's name is Jacob. He's my favorite cousin." Rayne waved her hand for me to say more. I must have sounded stupid. "Jacob and I are the same age and I've always been close to him."

Lydia handed me a card with a website address. "Fill out an application online. You'll need to list three references."

"Okay, thanks."

"WALK WITH ME OVER TO THE UNIVERSITY," Rayne said when we were outside.

I took a deep breath and looked around. The leaves on the trees seemed greener and the sky shone a brighter blue. Across the street, a catalpa tree sparkled with a cascade of white blossoms.

"I'm not sure about references. I'll choose my favorite teacher, Señor Martinez, but I don't know who else."

"Me, of course." Rayne put on a pair of oversize sunglasses.

"But you hardly know me."

"Don't worry, I'm on your side. Did you have Reinertsen for biology?"

"Yeah." My face was reflected in her glasses.

"Put him down. He gives excellent recommendations."

"He won't remember me."

"That doesn't matter. He doesn't remember most students, but he always gives glowing recommendations."

"How do you know this stuff?"

"I pay attention." She crossed the street and I hurried to keep up. "What will you put down for work experience?"

I told her about the country club.

"Yuck." She made a face like she couldn't imagine a worse job. "Did you work with anybody there with a disability?"

"No." I shook my head.

"None of the busboys or dishwashers?"

"Oh, yeah, Kevin, one of the dishwashers. He was the hardest worker and has been there for years. I don't even think of him that way."

"Good answer. Put that down."

"Why are you so eager for me to get this job?" I sounded a bit paranoid.

"If someone offers you help, take it." She punched me lightly on the shoulder. "Besides, you've got good energy. I'm looking out for myself, too. I don't want to share this job with some tight-ass."

AFTER RAYNE WENT OFF TO THE ART DEPARTMENT, I returned home to fill out the application on my laptop, confident nobody else would be there. The first questions were easy—basic information about myself and the position I was applying for. I paused at the one about days available and then checked all of them to show how eager I was. For the question about how I learned about the job, I answered honestly. *From Rayne.*

The one section I got stuck on was education. There were boxes for the names of schools, degrees, majors, and scholastic honors. That obviously meant college, and I was stumped about what to put down. In the end, I just listed my elementary, middle, and high school, which looked super lame.

I filled out the references and the employment history and made a point to list Kevin as one of my coworkers. Maybe I made it sound like we worked together more closely than we did, but it was a job application, after all. I finished up with a couple of easy questions about possessing a valid driver's license and not having ever been convicted of a felony. I checked it over, made a couple of small changes, and sent it in.

An hour later, while I was staring at videos on my laptop, my phone buzzed.

"Cray, this is Lydia at CSS, Clairemont Support Services. We'd like you to come in for an interview. Are you free tomorrow morning at ten?"

"Yes, yes, absolutely." Finally something good. Something that came directly from Rayne.

AFTER SOME HOOPS AT THE PARK, I went home for dinner. I hadn't seen Mom or Dad since the college confrontation because I hadn't wanted to go back until I had a good shot at a job.

"Did you find work?" Dad zeroed in as soon as I sat down at the big rectangular table in the dining room. The room, as usual, was spotless thanks to the cleaning service.

I scooped up some lettuce and avocado. "I've got an interview with a social services agency tomorrow."

"Which one?" Dad ground pepper on his salad. He didn't allow salt at the table because of his high blood pressure, so he compensated by using plenty of pepper.

"CSS, Clairemont Support Services. They run programs for adults with disabilities."

Mom handed me a basket of warm crescent rolls. "How'd you hear about this job?"

"My friend Rayne works there."

"Rayne." Lansing looked up. "That's a peculiar name. As if it's raining."

"Like you should talk, Lansing."

"That's enough, boys," Mom interrupted. "What's Rayne's last name?"

I paused. It hadn't come up. "I don't know."

"She's your friend and you don't know her last name?" Lansing said.

It was strange how we were talking about the job and Rayne, but we weren't talking about college. Dad must have told Mom and Lansing not to bring it up, and I was suspicious. He attacked his chicken and I tried to guess what scheme he had to make me do what he wanted. It was like trying to stay one step ahead in a video game, but in this case, it wasn't a game. It was my life.

"What kind of job?" Dad asked while he chewed.

"An overnight position where I'd be responsible for the house."

"You'd stay up all night?" Mom said. "I don't like that."

"Actually, I'd sleep. I'd be there in case of emergencies."

Dad put his fork down and stared at me. "That's not a job. A job is one where you get up in the morning and go to work. It's not a place to sleep."

"It's a job. I'd get paid." My chest tightened.

"Is it full-time?" Mom asked.

"Part-time. Three nights a week."

"You need a real full-time job." Dad's face flushed with anger. "Not some half-assed sleeping job."

Across the table, Lansing tried to hide a smile, and I wanted to kick him.

"You're the one playing games with college, so you're the one who needs to earn money for rent." Dad's face got redder. "You're creating this situation, not us, so you're going to live with the consequences."

"I didn't make up the rules."

"They're for your benefit," Dad shouted.

I looked down. That was total bullshit.

"I'm doing this for your own good so you see what life's like in the real world. You have an unbelievable opportunity with college and need to change your mind. I'm doing you a favor. You may not like it now, but you'll thank me later."

I pushed chicken around my plate.

Yeah, right. I wasn't thanking him. What he wanted was for him, not for me. I'd never seen that more clearly.

INDEPENDENT LIVING

THE NEXT MORNING, my phone buzzed. It was Jett.

"Hey, Cray Man, you awake?"

"Am now. What's up?"

"Nora's folks were out of town last night so I stayed over at her place. I'm just leaving now."

"Wow." I stuffed a pillow behind my head.

"She's wild, way different from what everybody thinks. I didn't sleep at all and I'll pay for it at camp today, but it was completely worth it."

"You finally got her." Knowing what he wanted had paid off.

"Yep." Jett laughed. "What's up with you?"

"Rayne lined up an interview for me. I told her I needed a job and she knew about one."

"Where?"

"A place called Oakcrest. Get this: I'd be paid to sleep."

"No way."

"That's what Rayne does, and I'd work the nights she doesn't."

"I thought being paid to hoop was good. Paid to sleep—that's unreal."

"Yeah. I'll let you know how it goes. Hey, what are you doing tonight?"

"Going bowling with Nora. Why don't you ask someone and join us?"

"I don't know." I couldn't think of anybody but then got a crazy idea. "I'll ask Rayne."

"That won't work," Jett said. "Ask someone else."

"What's the matter with Rayne?"

"She won't want to bowl."

"I'll let you know." I set the phone down and wondered why he didn't want me asking her.

I fell back to sleep, but my phone woke me up again. This time it was a number I didn't know. "Hello?" I sat up.

"It's me, Rayne. What are you doing?"

"Nothing." I was glad to hear her voice but confused why she was calling.

"Meet me at the edge in fifteen minutes."

"The edge of what?" I got up and opened my shades to the light.

"The Edge Coffee Shop."

"Oh." I struggled to think clearly. "Why?"

"To prep for your interview." She talked quickly. "Do you have a picture of you and Jacob?"

"I think so."

"Bring it with you. See you in fifteen minutes."

Fifteen minutes. Not enough time to shower. I scrambled into my bathroom, blasted body spray, and patted down my hair. Then I pictured Rayne's stuck-out 'do and stopped. Maybe neat hair wasn't important for this job.

Everything was quiet downstairs. Mom and Dad were already at work and Lansing had left a note saying he and a friend had gone to the science museum.

I burst into Mom's office, where she had a board full of photos. I picked one of Jacob with our family. It wasn't exactly right, but it would have to do. I pulled pins from the picture and then remembered another.

In the living room, I opened the drawer where Mom kept my baby scrapbook and found the picture I wanted: me and Jacob as babies holding onto each other in a bubble bath. Mom's caption said we were both ten months old. The picture was glued down with a sparkly silver border and I couldn't rip it out, so I put the newer picture inside the scrapbook, shoved it all in my backpack, and biked down to the Edge.

"HEY," I said to Rayne, who sat at her usual table eating a muffin. From her look of pleasure, I could tell it was wheat-free. She wore a sleeveless turquoise top that showed off her toned arms.

"For you." She pushed a plate forward with a blueberry scone on it.

"Thanks." I took a bite.

"I've got to be at work in thirty minutes, and I wanted to prep you for Gail and Stephanie." Rayne sipped her tea.

"Who are they?"

"Gail's the program director and Stephanie's the house supervisor. Gail's okay. She's hyper rule-oriented and comes off tougher than she is. She's got a son with Down syndrome. That's how she got into the field. The picture of your cousin will help. You've got it?"

I lifted the book onto the table and opened it. "Here's one from when I was a baby." I was embarrassed about Mom's over-the-top scrapbooking decorations.

Rayne leaned over and stared at the picture. "Beautiful. He's beautiful. You're beautiful."

"Thanks." It felt odd accepting a compliment on how I looked as a baby, but I was happy to take anything from her.

She paged through the pictures of me. "You're lucky to have this."

"Yeah." I'd never thought of Mom's scrapbooking that way.

"And who do we have here?" Rayne pushed forward the recent picture. "This must be Jacob."

"Yeah, and my mom, dad, and brother."

"Tell me about them," she said.

I talked about how extreme and controlling Dad was and how Mom always backed him up and how Lansing did exactly what they expected. Rayne listened and seemed to absorb everything.

I even told her about them picking my college and what I was going to study and me not going along with it and them being mad and Dad making me pay rent to live at home.

"You had to do it. That's one of the stupidest things I've ever heard."

"I'm not sure what I want, but I know I don't want to be a doctor."

"That's big. Knowing what you don't want is the first step in knowing what you do. Some people never get to that point."

"Yeah, I like that." I sat back and felt like I was getting credit for what I'd done. "I can't let them decide my life."

"Of course not." She shook her head slowly. "Parents can be the biggest disappointments on the planet."

I kept talking, like a dam had burst and the water was flooding downstream. "Dad's angry and Mom's disappointed and I know they both expect me to change my mind and accept their deal, but I'm not going to. Absolutely not." I'd never been so honest with anyone about what was going on in my family, and telling her made me feel more confident.

"We're both not going to college in the fall." She held out her fist. "We're gappers together."

I bumped my fist against hers and smiled.

She glanced at the clock and I waited to hear what else she'd say.

"Independent living."

"What?" I moved forward.

"That's the key."

"The key to what?"

"Independent living is the key to your interview. If you're ever in doubt about an answer, say independent living, people living as independently as possible. Stephanie's huge on that. Just remember independent living and be yourself."

My head was swimming.

"I've got to go." She gathered up her journal and shoved it in her backpack. "Show those pictures right away and fix your bed-head hair."

I stood and kind of waved as she went out. Rayne was incredible. She knew what to do about everything.

INTERVIEWING

LATER THAT MORNING, I sat in a worn chair facing Lydia's desk, waiting to be called. My right heel tapped a mile a minute even when I put my hand on the clean khakis I'd worn to make a good impression.

Independent living. Be yourself. Rayne's advice echoed in my head.

I stared down at the scrapbook. When I was little, I used to ask Mom to go through it because I liked hearing stories about how excited she and Dad were when I was born, but I hadn't looked at it in years.

I opened to a picture of Mom holding me at the hospital with Dad leaning in, both beaming like the proudest parents in the world. They looked so young, not that much older than me. I couldn't imagine being a parent.

I paged through pictures of me, Mom, Dad, and later Lansing. Dad's smile faded as I got bigger. Maybe when I was a baby, he could imagine me the way he wanted, but as I got older, I kept falling short of his expectations.

"Crayton." Lydia looked up. "Gail and Stephanie are ready for you."

I closed the scrapbook. *Be yourself.* What if I wasn't sure who that was?

Two women stood up in the conference room.

"Hi, I'm Stephanie, the house supervisor at Oakcrest." She had wavy blond hair and big hoop earrings.

"And I'm Gail," a woman with square-framed glasses said. "I'm the program director."

"Nice to meet you. I'm Cray." I sat down across from them.

"Let's get right to it." Gail had a no-nonsense manner that suddenly reminded me of my third-grade teacher, Ms. Carling, who complained to Mom that my worksheets were messy. "Why do you want to join the Oakcrest team?"

I was tempted to say because I needed a job, but I followed Rayne's instructions and pushed the scrapbook forward. I opened to the bubble-bath picture and talked about how close Jacob and I were and how he collected Batman stuff and he'd be Robin and I'd be Batman. I told them I didn't think of him as having a disability, just different abilities, and Stephanie nodded.

"Why are you applying for the three-month, part-time night position at Oakcrest?" Gail asked.

"Rayne recommended it to me." I knew I needed to say more. "I'm responsible and think I could do a good job."

Gail frowned. That wasn't what she wanted to hear.

"What areas of interest do you have in working with our adults?" Stephanie asked.

"Independent living. I think people should live as independently as possible."

Stephanie glowed like I'd hit the jackpot.

"You recently graduated from high school." Gail looked down at her paper. "What are your plans for the fall?"

"I want to gain some work experience."

"What about college?" she asked.

"I'm not going right away."

"Why not?"

There was no way I was telling her about Dad. "Developing new skills will make my college application stronger." I was making stuff up and it sounded that way. Then I remembered what Rayne had called it. "I'm taking a gap year."

"Do you have any questions for us?" Stephanie asked.

Rayne hadn't mentioned me asking questions, so I thought quickly. *Independent living.* "How do you help people at Oakcrest become more independent?"

Stephanie talked about a person-centered approach with individual action plans and specific goals. She said everybody in the house had a job, and she listed them. I couldn't keep it all straight, but I was happy to be listening rather than talking.

"Do you have any other questions?" Gail asked.

"When does the job start?"

"Soon." Gail straightened the papers in front of her. "We need the position filled, but we have to make sure we choose the right person. If you were selected, when could you begin?"

"Immediately."

Gail wrote something down on her paper. "We'll keep you posted."

"Thank you." I couldn't tell how I'd done.

"Thanks, Cray." Stephanie stood up. She came around the table and shook my hand, but Gail stayed where she was.

I worried I'd made a mistake as I picked up my stuff. "Thank you, Gail."

"We have your contact info." She didn't look up.

AT HOME, I felt like I'd blown it after being so confident. I wasn't going to work with Rayne after all. I wondered if Stephanie and Gail had to agree. If they did, then I wasn't getting hired.

I desperately needed to talk to Rayne and tried to remember where she worked at the university. I changed into shorts and a T-shirt, then grabbed a granola bar from the cupboard and headed over to campus. I called Jett but he didn't answer. They probably couldn't have phones on at camp.

The art department. That's what she'd said. I waited for the traffic to clear and darted across the street. A guy with a full beard and a ponytail sat waiting for the campus bus.

"Do you know where the art department is?"

"One block, take a right, and cross the bridge. New building with dark glass. You can't miss it."

"Thanks." I hurried off. I jumped out of the way of a sprinkler head that popped up and started spraying and wiped my face. My phone buzzed, and I pulled it out. "Hi, Rayne."

"You got it, Crayster."

"What?"

"You got the job," she said excitedly.

"No. You're kidding."

"I was just talking to Stephanie about scheduling and she told me. She was impressed by your commitment to independent living. Gail was hesitant, but Stephanie persuaded her to give you a shot."

"What was Gail's problem?"

"She's big on hiring people with degrees. She thinks a staff with lots of college grads is more professional, and she didn't like that you didn't have plans for the fall."

"Join the club. She can talk with my parents about that."

"Stephanie liked you and that's what counts. She's the house supervisor and Gail knows she runs excellent houses."

It was slowly sinking in that I had a job. "Thanks, Rayne."

"It's nothing."

"No, I really needed this. Thanks."

"Then you're welcome."

"One more question." I walked faster. "Do you like to bowl?"

"What?"

"Do you want to go bowling tonight?" I climbed the cement steps of the bridge.

"Sure. Bowling's a blast."

"Great." Jett was totally wrong about that.

"Where are you? It sounds windy."

"I'm on the bridge crossing over to the art department."

"You're here now? Come up to room 323."

LIKE ANY OTHER HOUSE

A JOB, a job, I've got a job. The inside of the building was dark after I'd been in the sun, but the AC felt cool. I rode the elevator to the third floor and followed the numbers. *I've got a job.*

I turned the corner and Rayne was waiting with her arms outstretched. "Way to go, Crayster."

"Thanks." She gave me a strong hug, not one of those turn-to-the-side or lean-way-forward ones that some girls give.

"They want you to start as soon as you can."

"Really? You're not messing with me?" I looked into her brown eyes.

She shook her head. "I wouldn't do that to you."

I was so lucky to have met her. She was smart and different and knew how to make things happen.

"Welcome to my world." She opened a door and led me to a neatly arranged counter. "I'm not supposed to have visitors, but it's okay this once."

Nearby tables contained stacks of photographs. Around the

room, the walls were lined with framed black-and-white portraits, landscapes, and city scenes. "You like photography?"

"I love it," she said, "but I also love drawing, design, writing, history, biology, philosophy. When I do go to college, I have to figure out a way to combine it all."

I noticed a nameplate on her desk: RAYNE MACCRIMMON. I repeated the last name to myself, the one I hadn't known when Mom asked. A new large-screen Mac, an extra monitor, a high-end scanner, and stacks of files also sat on her desk. Rayne's job was so different from those of most high school students. So was her night job, my new job.

"I liked Stephanie." I picked up a rubber band and stretched it.

"She's the best," Rayne said. "You'll learn so much from her."

"Gail's not that friendly." I slipped the band around my wrist.

"Don't worry. Once you start, you'll hardly ever see her. Stephanie runs the house."

I moved around the room, glancing at photographs. "Do you work here by yourself?"

"Yes. I've got a supervisor, Professor Murphy, who checks on me. She insists I call her Murph and brings me books she thinks I'll like. Other than that, I'm on my own. She shows me what needs to be done and I do it."

"Cool." I stopped in front of a photograph of two men rolling dice against a brick wall. "I'm glad we're going bowling tonight."

"Me too." Rayne pretended to bowl an imaginary ball.

"I hope it's okay we're going with a couple of other people."

"Who?" She looked concerned.

"Jett and Nora."

"That seriously sucks." Rayne shook her head and walked to her desk.

"What?" I was surprised at her sudden mood change.

"Nora and I hate each other."

"Why?" I'd thought of Rayne as more a peace-and-love person.

"She's dishonest and uses people. Last fall, she talked about me behind my back, so I confronted her. She accused me of being different just to be different. I asked her what the problem was with that and why it was her business. I quoted John Stuart Mill about eccentricity abounding when strength and character abound, and Nora accused me of showing off." Rayne picked up a paper clip and bent it. "This from Nora, who's planned to be valedictorian since sixth grade."

I knew Nora well enough to know she probably worried that Rayne was smarter than she was. Still, I was surprised to hear they hated each other.

"Since then, I avoid her. She brings people down."

"It's just bowling," I said. "We can be on the same team. Wouldn't you like to beat her?"

"Maybe. She's probably a terrible bowler. But I hate being around her."

My phone buzzed. "Hello."

"This is Stephanie. I've got good news, Cray. We'd like to offer you the Oakcrest job."

"Great." I pretended not to know.

Rayne gave me a thumbs-up and started typing away on her keyboard.

"When can you come to the house for an introduction?" Stephanie asked.

"Anytime."

"I'm here now while everybody is at work. Can you come over?"

"Sure. Where is it?"

She gave me a nearby address. I ended the call and looked over at Rayne. "I'm going to see the house."

"I know. Stephanie told me earlier."

"What about bowling?" I looked at her and hoped she could tell how much I wanted her to say yes.

"Okay. Let's crush 'em."

I APPROACHED A BROWN SPLIT-LEVEL HOUSE ON A street lined with oak trees. A new blue Prius sat in the driveway.

I rang the bell and Stephanie greeted me. "Welcome to Oakcrest. I'm so glad you'll be working with us, Cray." She handed me a set of keys. "The square one is for the front door, the round one is for the back, and the small one is for the patio door."

"Thank you." I climbed the carpeted stairs and admired the wide-open layout of the house.

"I've got some forms you need to fill out." She handed me a folder. "Get them back to me as soon as you can."

I opened it and noticed the one on top: Criminal Background Check. I'd fill it out later.

"This is the living room," she said. "Obviously."

Two dark couches, two matching chairs, and a big TV screen made the room feel comfortable. On one of the chairs, a black cat stretched.

"Who's this?" I walked over.

"That's Chimney, the house cat. Kate picked the name, and Chimney sleeps with her, but everybody takes turns feeding him and cleaning out the litter box."

I reached down, but the cat jumped off and raced out of the room.

"Here's the house computer." Stephanie showed me a laptop on the counter. "Individual action plans, med changes, staff logs, everything you need to know."

Individual action plans, med changes. Suddenly it hit me that the job wasn't going to be as simple as being paid to sleep.

"The dining room." Stephanie extended her arm. "Dinner is eaten inside or out on the deck depending on what people prefer." She slid open the glass door and showed me the gas grill and new patio furniture.

"Nice." A couple of big oaks provided plenty of shade.

She straightened the cushions on a chair. "We want to be part of the neighborhood, just like any other house."

We went back into the kitchen, which had granite countertops, shiny appliances, and dark wooden cupboards.

"The people we support take turns doing the cooking." She picked up a box of Pop-Tarts and put it back in the cupboard. "The evening staff person assists with skill development, and our goal, as you know, is to have people be as independent as possible."

As I looked around the kitchen, I liked how different it felt, not like some job at the mall.

Stephanie walked me down the hallway. "The four bedrooms are all here. This is Nicole's." She stopped in front of a door whose every square inch was covered with Justin Bieber posters.

"She's into music."

"She's into Justin Bieber." Stephanie smiled. "Nicole's outgoing and will talk to anybody she meets. She struggles with paying attention sometimes and in groups has a tendency to wander off."

She moved on. "This is Sean's room. He loves to dance and tell jokes, sometimes as a way of covering up what he doesn't understand. He's also into shampoo and has a habit of stealing it from others."

"Really?"

"Yes, he's got quite the collection." Stephanie stopped in front of another door.

"This room is Kate's. She can be anxious and will bite her arm when she's wound up. She'll be suspicious of you, but don't take it personally, and give her time."

I'd never heard of anybody biting her own arm. I noticed a little cat door in the bottom of Kate's door. It was hard to picture people without meeting them or seeing inside their rooms. "Can we look in?"

Stephanie shook her head. "No, we need to respect privacy." She pointed to the last door. "That's Brent's room. He's close to Rebecca, the staff person you'll be subbing for. Brent's an extraordinary man. He's had seizures his whole life and has an unsteady gait, but he works harder at being independent than anybody I know, and he's gone further than we expected."

"Sounds like an interesting group."

"It is," Stephanie said. "When done well, this job looks easy. But be aware, it's hard work to get to that point. Can you come for supper tomorrow night and meet everybody?"

"Sure. What time?"

"Six. I'll be here as well, and we'll pay you for your orientation hours. Any questions or concerns?"

I considered telling her that I got faint around blood but decided that wasn't necessary. "No, I don't think so."

"One more thing." We went downstairs to an open room in a finished basement. "This is where you'll sleep." In front of us was a full-size bed with floral pillows and a light-green bedspread.

Beside it on a table sat a book titled *Discover Skye*. "In this closet are clean sheets and pillowcases. You'll strip the bed on the last morning of your shift and put on clean sheets the first night you work."

I stared at the neatly made bed. That was where Rayne slept, where I would sleep. I felt myself getting excited. For my new job, I got to share a bed with Rayne.

IT'S DIFFERENT

"I GOT THE JOB," I announced as I walked into the house.

"Good for you." Mom cut up a cucumber at the kitchen island. Beside her, Lansing sliced a red pepper.

I pulled a Gatorade from the inside door of the fridge. "I'm going out tonight. Can I borrow your car?"

"Where are you going and with whom?"

"Bowling with Jett, Nora, and Rayne." I unscrewed the cap and took a drink.

"I guess that's fine. Don't be late."

"So you're really not enrolling at St. Luke's?" Lansing asked.

"Yeah." I took a cuke slice off Mom's cutting board and popped it in my mouth.

"Are you planning on living here forever?"

"Shut up." I glared at him.

"That's enough." Mom set her knife down and wiped her hands on a towel. "Cray, I want you to understand something. I know you think your father's being tough on you. He's a complicated man, but he cares deeply and is concerned about your future. He's worked hard to be successful and he wants the same for you. Believe me, I know how traditional he is and how difficult that can be sometimes, but he wants you to be a doctor, partly as a way to stay connected."

"There are other ways to do that." I turned to Lansing. "You're going to do it, right?"

"Sure; I want to be a surgeon."

"He doesn't need both of us." I took another cuke. "I want to study what I choose, not what Dad wants."

"You can be premed and still study other things." She pulled a package of salmon out of the refrigerator. "What about being a pediatrician? You're good with kids. We need more pediatricians."

"I don't want to be a doctor. How many times do I have to say it?"

"You probably don't know this, Cray, but one of the reasons this is so important to your father is what happened to Stevie. He never talks about it, but I know it weighs on him."

"Who?" I turned around.

"Stevie. Stephen, your father's younger brother."

"What happened to him again?" Lansing asked.

I took a gulp of Gatorade. I wasn't even born when Stevie had his accident.

"Stevie was fun and funny, but a bit of a lost soul," she said. "He drifted around Europe and couldn't figure out what he wanted. He ended up on some farm with a bunch of odd people in Scotland."

I finished off my Gatorade. This had nothing to do with me. I wasn't going to live on a farm.

"One day he spent the afternoon at a pub. I'm sure he had plenty to drink, and when he got in his car, he started driving in the right lane, the one we drive in here, but the wrong one there.

Another driver came over the hill, didn't see him, and smashed into him. He was killed instantly."

I shook my head. "So if I don't agree to go to St. Luke's and be a doctor, I'll be killed in a head-on crash. That's what you're saying?"

"No." She held up her hand. "But you need to think seriously about what you're doing. You need to have a plan. Being a doctor is a good life. You wouldn't believe the number of people who come up to your father and thank him for what he's done for them." She picked up the salmon package and sliced it open. "We just want what's best for you."

"No, you don't. Dad wants to maintain the family tradition, and you want to tell people both your sons are going to be doctors."

"That's enough." She pointed the knife at me. "You're the one who let us believe you were enrolling at St. Luke's when you weren't and kept it secret. That was dishonest, a major betrayal."

I rinsed the empty Gatorade bottle and threw it in the recycling bin. I saw Lansing staring at me with big eyes.

"And now we're not even having your graduation party since you're not going to college. The whole thing is humiliating. I'm disappointed in you. I expected much more." Mom shook the knife. "Why are you being so stubborn about this?"

"Me being stubborn?" I raised my voice. "You and Dad are the ones being stubborn."

"You're more like him than you realize." She slammed the knife on the cutting board.

"I am not!" I grabbed the extra set of Audi keys from the holder.

"You both refuse to give in when you think you're right. Believe me, you're a lot like him."

"Don't ever say that again!" I stormed out.

"Be careful," she called after me.

I tried to leave her words floating in the air, but they chased after.

Be careful. Be careful. Be careful.

I RACED DOWN THE STREET IN THE CAR. *Disappointed.* I hated it when she said that, like I was a complete failure. *Betrayal* wasn't fair either. Yeah, I should have told them earlier about deciding not to go to St. Luke's. But they would have gone crazy and tried to force me to do it. I didn't want to end high school that way.

But saying I was like Dad was the worst thing she could say. I wasn't like him at all. I blasted music to drown out my thoughts.

When I pulled up to an old three-story brick building on a bumpy, cobblestoned street on the other side of the river, I thought I'd made a mistake. It looked like an abandoned factory, not a house.

I turned down the volume and checked the address Rayne had given me: 109 Canal Avenue. I couldn't see any numbers or tell where the door was. I got out and looked around. At that moment, Rayne appeared from a metal door and came down the loading dock carrying a canvas bag.

"Hey, you look great."

"Thanks." She wore flip-flops, long, flowing pants, and an orange silk top with a dark bra.

"What's in the bag?"

"Bowling shoes." She pulled them out proudly. "I went down to Goodwill this afternoon and they had this one pair exactly my size. I still don't like getting together with Nora, but I'm pleased with these."

I opened the passenger door. "Interesting place."

"What do you mean?" She sat down and gathered the bottom of her pants to make sure they were out of the door as I closed it.

"I mean it's different." I got in and started the car.

"Different from what?" she said sharply. "Different from your house? Different from what a house should be?"

"No, I didn't mean it that way. I like it."

She slumped back in the seat as we drove in silence, and I tried to figure out what was going on.

"I hate people saying it's different." She stared out the window. "Usually that means they don't like something but don't have the balls to say it. Different is fine. Different is good. We need more different. We have way too much the same around here."

"I agree. I really do."

We stopped at a red light next to a bearded guy on a motorcycle. He had a collie wearing a small helmet in a sidecar.

I was on the verge of saying, *Now, that's different*, but caught myself. "That's cool."

Rayne nodded.

The guy revved his motorcycle and raced off. I made a note for the future: Rayne could be touchy about being labeled different.

JETT AND NORA WERE AT THE BOWLING ALLEY WHEN we arrived, and Jett gave Rayne a hug while Nora cleaned a pink bowling ball with an antibacterial wipe. She waved halfheartedly. "Hi, Rayne."

"Hey." Rayne sat down and put on her orange-and-green Goodwill specials.

I said hello and went up to the counter to pay and get shoes.

"Those are different," Nora said, pointing to Rayne's shoes.

"Oh, do you like them?" Rayne asked.

"Sure," she said, and I could see what Rayne had meant. It was obvious Nora didn't.

Jett followed me. "I got a strange call from your dad today."

"About what?"

"He wanted me to persuade you to go to St. Luke's. Even when I told him I couldn't and it was your decision, he insisted I try."

I shook my head. Going behind my back to Jett was pathetic.

"He said to keep it a secret, so don't tell him that I told you."

"I won't, but he's a jerk to do that."

When we started bowling, Rayne glided up to the line and her pants flowed out behind her. Rather than watching her blue ball, I watched her. But then I heard the clatter of pins. She'd knocked them all down. She raised her arms and grinned, and I was glad to be on her team.

The other surprise, though, was Nora. She was good, too. It turned out she bowled with her grandpa, and she matched Rayne with strikes and spares.

Jett and I were even, so the game stayed tight. Early on, it shifted from bowling for fun to winning. Jett hated to lose and so did I, but Nora and Rayne were super competitive. They watched each other closely and kept an eye on the score. On our last frame, we were down by nine and it was up to me. I needed my best roll of the night.

I took my black ball out of the rack and tried to relax.

"Visualize a strike," Rayne called.

I stepped forward. The lane seemed narrower and the pins looked far away. I tried to imagine all of them tumbling but couldn't. *Remember to follow through.* I moved to the line and let the ball go.

It looked good as it struck the pins. Six went down, seven, eight, then nine. The tenth one wobbled, but it balanced and stayed up. One lonely pin on the left side next to the gutter to knock down for the win.

"Way to go, Crayster!" Rayne rushed up and hugged me.

"Sorry, Cray." Nora stood up. "That was a foul."

"What?" I turned and stared.

"Your foot was an inch over the line." Nora pointed. "Wasn't it, Jett?"

He shrugged. "I guess."

"No, it wasn't."

"You don't call a foul when we're bowling for fun," Rayne protested.

"It's the rules. If your foot crosses the line, you get a zero." Nora adjusted her bra strap.

"What's the matter with you?" Rayne started toward her.

Jett stepped between them. "Hey, wait. How about a do-over?"

"You can't have a do-over on a foul," Nora insisted. "Those are the official rules."

Jett avoided looking at me. He wasn't challenging her even though she was way out of line.

"It's the rules," Nora repeated.

"I don't care," I said. "You can't call that."

Rayne picked up her blue ball and flung it down the lane. It cracked the remaining pin solidly. She grabbed up her flip-flops, shoved them in her bag, and reached for my hand. "Let's get the hell out of here."

GONE

"SEE WHAT I MEAN?" Rayne said. "She's a manipulating liar."

"Sorry I suggested it." I started the car.

"She runs that crap on everybody, and one person after another backs down. What's the matter with Jett? I hate to see him with her. Why didn't he say something?"

"I don't know."

"Because he's scared of her. She's the hot blond girl going to Stanford, and he can't believe she's sleeping with him. Some guys lose their balls around girls like that. If there's one thing I can't stand it's guys without balls."

I made another mental note: *Hang on to my balls.*

"What about Sam's for pizza?"

Rayne shook her head. "Wheat, remember?"

"Oh, right. No pizza, no pasta—where do you go?"

"There's a Thai place across the street from the post office. Do you like Thai food?"

"Anything. I'm starving."

"You would have knocked that last pin down and we would

have won. That's why Nora did that." Rayne slapped the dash-board. "And Jett went along with her like she was a dictator."

I'd never seen Rayne like this. I thought of her as more calm and under control, but this side of her was kind of exciting.

"Do you understand now why I won't be around her?"

"Yeah, definitely." That had to be the reason Jett hadn't wanted me to ask Rayne. "You bowled great, though."

"You think so? I haven't done it in a long time, and smashing that last pin was satisfying. And I love these shoes. I can wear them for more than bowling."

Images of what that could be flashed in my mind.

RAYNE CHOSE TO SIT NEXT TO ME AT THE RESTAURANT, rather than on the other side of the table. "Everybody sits across from each other," she said. "There's no law that says you have to."

I opened the menu. Doing everything differently could get to be a lot of work. "Do you want to start with egg rolls?"

"Wheat," she said. "We could have vegetarian spring rolls."

"What are spring rolls?"

"Like egg rolls, but with a rice-flour wrap and not deep fried. They're good here."

"As good as egg rolls?" I stopped my heel tapping since I was right beside her.

"You can get egg rolls."

"No, I want something we both can eat."

We ordered spring rolls, and I chose chicken pad Thai while Rayne got green curry with tofu.

"You don't eat meat either, do you?"

"No wheat, no meat," Rayne said. "I'm difficult."

"But you're okay with me ordering it?"

"Yeah," she said. "I think the way meat's produced is obscene and that people who eat it put their health in jeopardy and that the planet would be in better shape if people ate less meat, but I respect other people's choices."

"You're trying to make me feel guilty."

"A little." She smiled. Her smile was cool. It wasn't one of those over-the-top, teeth-flashing smiles. It was subtle, more real. "I like guys who don't eat meat."

"Really?"

"Absolutely. They smell better." She stated it definitively, like it was a well-known scientific fact.

I got the waitress's attention and changed my order to tofu.

"You don't have to," Rayne said.

"I know." I wasn't sure if what she'd said was true, but I wasn't taking a chance on smelling bad.

Rayne got up to use the bathroom and I did, too. I looked at my face in the mirror, and I didn't look sad, like I had in the picture she'd drawn. I looked excited, like I couldn't wait to get back to see what would happen next.

The waitress set down the spring rolls and peanut sauce. Rayne picked one up with her chopsticks and set it on my plate. "Enjoy."

I examined it. Veggies inside a soft roll. "This looks like something that's good for you."

"It is." Rayne dipped hers in peanut sauce and took a bite.

I chewed a corner and it tasted like grass and twigs.

"Delicious, isn't it?" Rayne licked her lips.

"I need sauce." I spooned some onto my plate.

"I heard you're starting your orientation," Rayne said.

"I'm having dinner at the house tomorrow."

"I know. You'll meet Eli, who works weekends. You'll like him. He went to art school for a couple of years but is taking time off to concentrate on his music. He plays guitar and sings with a fun band."

I took another bite of the spring roll. It was weird how Rayne knew everything before I did.

AFTER WE ATE, Rayne said it would be a good night to check out the view from Croton Hill. I moved lightly along the path, excited to be alone with her.

Rayne scurried over a fallen tree.

"Nice shoes."

"I told you these would be good for more than bowling. I wouldn't want to do this in flip-flops."

"Absolutely." I liked her in those goofy shoes.

At the top, rather than looking over the city, Rayne led me the other way. A little path wound down around rocks and trees to a different view, one of a big bend in the river.

"Everybody goes to the other side to see the lights, but this is better." Rayne sat on a ledge. "It's more peaceful."

I sat down next to her and looked out at the water. I'd done some stuff with girls, but never anybody like Rayne. I didn't know where things were headed, but it felt significant, less like being in high school and more like real life. I reached out my hand, but she pulled hers back. "What's the matter?"

"There's something you need to know."

"What?"

"My mom's gone."

"What do you mean?" I wanted her to face me, but she kept staring straight ahead.

"My brother and I live with my dad. My mom split when we were little. We don't see her."

I swallowed and thought about what to say.

"Plenty of people can't handle it." Rayne finally turned toward to me. "I need to know up front."

"I can handle it." I looked directly at her and felt like I was making a pledge. I felt strong saying it, though I didn't know what it would require. I wanted to kiss her at that moment, but it didn't seem right after she'd just pulled her hand away.

A million questions popped into my mind. I knew Rayne wouldn't want me freaking out and asking them, though, so I played it cool. I didn't need to know everything right away, but one question felt okay to ask. "What's your brother's name?"

"Aaron," Rayne said.

"I like that name." I was dying to reach out and hold her, but that clearly wasn't what she wanted since her hands were squeezed between her knees and she was staring ahead like she was in a trance.

I focused on the bend in the river as the first stars came out. Everything with Rayne felt intense.

OAKCREST

SATURDAY AFTERNOON, Dad caught me in the kitchen munching Honey Nut Cheerios out of the box. "What do you think you're doing?"

"Eating breakfast." I wanted to call him out about going behind my back, but I'd promised Jett I wouldn't.

"What were you doing this morning?" He made himself another cup of coffee with his new Italian espresso machine.

"Sleeping." Asking questions he knew the answers to was one of his favorite tricks.

"Have you found a real job yet?"

"I'm starting my new one today. I've got orientation at six." I poured cereal into a blue-rimmed bowl and added milk.

"For what? Sleeping? How much orientation does that require?"

I sat down at the table. Sometimes the best thing to do was ignore him and hope he'd stop talking.

"Lansing is at the country club caddying. You should be setting an example for him, not the other way around."

"I'll find something else," I answered automatically.

"Listen." Dad sat down across from me. "Your mother says you think I'm being tough on you. My dad was much tougher on me."

"How?"

"He used a belt for discipline, for one thing. You've never had a belt used on you, have you?"

"No." I'd never heard this about Grandpa. Maybe that was one of the reasons Dad was so extreme.

"Your mother and I never even spanked you boys." He said it like he was proud, like it was an accomplishment.

Maybe he'd tried to be more different from his dad than I realized.

"I've been thinking." His tone softened. "As a doctor, you have a chance to make a significant impact. Most people respect and admire their doctor, and you deal with issues of life and death. What could be more important than that?"

I had no answer as I ate my cereal.

"Your mother and I planned to give you a car this summer for starting college."

A car? I looked up. I desperately needed a car.

"I've got a friend at St. Luke's who I spoke to yesterday about your situation. I asked him to keep your spot open while we figure this out. He said they're willing to do that, and they're eager to have you as a member of the incoming class." He clasped his hands like he was praying. "I'd like you to do it."

"Under what conditions?"

"The ones we discussed—a fully paid college education for you to be premed. You can take any other classes you want as well."

He expected me to cave that easily.

69

"And a new car. We can go out to the dealership and pick it out today," he said. "What do you think?"

"What dealership?"

"Your choice."

Different cars popped into my mind, but I couldn't do it. He wanted to buy me off.

"No." I watched his face fall. I was giving up a brand-new car, but if I said yes, I'd be doing what he wanted every single day for the rest of my life. I'd live my life for somebody else.

"People from all over the world dream of coming to the United States to be doctors. Here you are with everything being handed to you and you're turning it down. You're ruining your life, Cray. Can't you see that?" Dad shook his head sadly. I could tell he couldn't believe I hadn't gone for the car. "I don't know why it's so damn hard for you to accept help."

"You want to know why? Because it's not about what I want. It's what you and Mom want. You don't even bother to ask me."

"Yes, we do. Besides, you're seventeen. The frontal lobes of your brain are still developing—the part that governs conse-quences." Dad tapped his head. "Most kids don't know what they want at seventeen. They need help, and the best people to provide it are parents. That's all your mother and I are doing."

"No, it's not." It felt impossible for him to see my perspective. "I've got to make my own choices. I've got to find some things out for myself."

"Then do it." He stood up. "You can start by finding a real job to pay your way around here."

"I've got a job. I'm getting paid." I stood up, too.

"Sleeping over is not a real job. You need something full-time during the day."

I picked up my bowl and spoon, opened the dishwasher, and put them in. "What I do is never enough."

"That's not true." Dad raised his voice. "But in this case it is. What you're doing about college and your future isn't enough. It's nowhere close to enough."

"Whatever I do is never enough for you." I walked out and left him standing there.

WHEN I CLIMBED THE STEPS TO OAKCREST, a woman with short brown hair and big glasses opened the door before I even had a chance to knock. She was the same woman I'd seen at the concert earlier in the week.

"Hi, I'm Nicole. You must be the new sub."

"Yeah, I'm Cray." I was surprised by how old she looked up close, probably over forty.

"Do you like Justin Bieber?"

"Who doesn't?" I followed her up the stairs and looked around for Stephanie.

"He's here," Nicole yelled.

People streamed into the living room.

A chubby guy with a big grin and a red NASCAR T-shirt greeted me. "I'm Sean Reid." He was the dancer from the concert. "Do you like jokes?"

"Sure."

"What's the difference between broccoli and boogers?" he asked excitedly.

"Broccoli and boogers? I don't know."

"Kids don't eat broccoli." Sean laughed loudly, and he had one of those deep, rumbling laughs that made other people laugh.

"Oh, Sean, that is so disgusting." Nicole frowned.

"No, it's not. It's funny."

"I'm Brent." A big guy staggered over and shook my hand with a firm grip. He had dark hair, glasses, and patches of stubble he'd missed shaving.

"I'm Cray."

"That's a funny name."

"Yeah, I know."

"Over there, that's Kate." Nicole pointed to the couch where a woman with short blond hair sat frowning with her arms crossed. "She's shy."

"She's not shy," Brent said.

Kate grunted but I couldn't understand her.

"She says she's shy," Nicole said.

"Hi, Kate." I waved, but she looked away from me. All the people in the house were at least twice my age. It was hard to believe I was supposed to be in charge of them in case of an emergency.

"Hey, I'm Eli." A short guy with a goatee walked over but didn't make eye contact. "I work weekends."

"Hi." I looked around again and wondered why Stephanie wasn't here when she said she would be.

"Brent and Nicole are putting dinner together. Make yourself comfortable." Eli followed them into the kitchen.

I wasn't sure about him. Maybe I wasn't going to like Eli. Maybe Rayne would be wrong about something for once. I looked over at Kate, who continued frowning.

"Do you like card tricks?" Sean asked.

"Sure." The cat wandered in and I reached out to pet him but he scooted away.

"I'll get my cards."

I sat down in a chair by Kate, who turned and bit her arm, which freaked me out. "What's for supper?" I tried not to show it.

She ignored me as Chimney jumped up, but she stopped biting her arm to pet him. I didn't know what else to say and was relieved when Sean came back.

"Pick a card, any card," he said.

I chose the eight of clubs and showed it to Sean.

"No, no, you don't show it to me." He looked over at Kate. "He doesn't know anything."

She shook her head like I was hopeless.

The front door opened and Stephanie appeared. "Sorry I'm late. I had an emergency at another house."

"He pulled a card, but he showed it to me." Sean held it up. "He was supposed to keep it secret."

"Looks like you're settling in, Cray," she said. "I need to check in with Eli."

"When's Rebecca coming back? I miss her," I overheard Brent tell Stephanie in the kitchen.

"Shh," Stephanie whispered. "Not until September."

Sean stared at me with his mouth open. "Ray, Jay, that's a hard name to remember."

"Yeah," I said. "Maybe I should change it."

"To what?"

"I don't know." I looked at his shirt. "I could go with something completely different, something easy, like . . . Race Car."

"Race Car?" Sean burst out laughing his deep laugh.

"What's so funny?" Nicole came out to check.

"He said his name is Race Car." Sean started laughing again.

"Nicole, get back in here and finish the salad," Brent shouted.

"Race Car," Sean said. "That's what I'll call you."

"Time to eat. Everybody, wash up," Brent called.

Sean and Kate went off and I gathered the cards and stacked them neatly.

After they finished, I walked down to the bathroom. I scrubbed my hands with extra soap and thought about what Dad had said about a "real job." Oakcrest didn't feel like a real job, more like hanging out at a house and getting to know people. I wasn't sure how I'd do or if anybody would listen to me or what it would be like to work with Kate who didn't like me and bit her arm. I was supposed to be in charge in case of an emergency, but I didn't know what to do because nobody was telling me.

I dried my hands on a towel and looked in the mirror and saw some fear. I hadn't thought about it enough. I wasn't qualified for what I was getting into. Maybe I should have taken the offer of the new car and enrolled at St. Luke's, just like everybody else who was off to college.

ORIENTATING

"PASS THE CHICKEN," Nicole said when I sat down at the table.

"Please," Stephanie added.

"Please," Nicole repeated.

I reached out to take the plate of grilled chicken from Kate, who continued to look away, and handed it to Nicole.

"I started my new pills today," Brent announced.

"We know that," Nicole said.

"I wasn't telling you." Brent looked at her irritably. "I was telling Stephanie."

"That's good." Stephanie nodded.

"The nurse said they should make me shake less." Brent took a spoonful of rice and shook noticeably.

"I hope they work better than the old pills." Stephanie passed me the salad.

"Who still needs rice?" Eli held up the bowl.

"Kate does," Nicole said.

"No," Kate snapped.

"You don't have any on your plate." Nicole pointed.

"No rice."

"You used to like rice."

"Let's let Kate decide if she wants rice," Stephanie suggested. "She can make her own dinner decisions."

"I was just helping," Nicole said.

"I know," Stephanie said, "but Kate can do it."

I tried to figure out why Stephanie and Eli sometimes told people what to do and sometimes didn't.

"How come you have a scar by your eye?" Nicole asked.

I told the story about me and Jacob at the playground and was surprised by how sympathetic everybody was.

"Somebody didn't clean the litter box. It stinks," Brent said. "Whose turn is it?"

Nicole spun around to study a chart. "Sean's."

"No, it's not," Sean said. "Remember, I cleaned it out for you last week when it was full of poop, and you said you'd do it this week."

"This is dinnertime," Stephanie said. "Let's discuss it later."

"I left my shampoo in the bathroom this morning," Nicole reported. "And somebody stole it."

"Seeeeaaaaannnnn," everybody said together.

"Make sure that gets back to Nicole right after supper." Eli pointed at him.

"Why is six scared of seven?" Sean asked me.

"What?"

"No more jokes, Sean," Nicole said.

"Why is the number six scared of the number seven?" Sean ignored her.

"I don't know."

"Because seven ate nine," Sean said triumphantly. "Get it? Seven, eight, nine."

76

"That's good." I took a bite of chicken. It was dry, but I was hungry after not eating anything but cereal earlier.

"Don't encourage him." Nicole opened up her napkin. "He's always telling jokes."

"I like that one." Eli held the bowl of corn for Brent. "Where did you hear it?"

"At work. Keith, my manager, told me. He knows lots of jokes."

"Speaking of work." Stephanie turned to him. "How's your job going?"

"Keith says I'm doing outstanding." Sean sat up taller. "He says I'm his best worker."

"They must have bad workers," Brent mumbled.

"Where do you work?" I looked across at Sean.

"The McDonald's by the mall."

That was one of the places I couldn't get a job—the one where the manager asked how much experience I had in the food-service industry. That seemed like a different lifetime.

"I'm a cook," Sean said proudly.

"That's why I never eat there." Brent struggled to cut his chicken but worked diligently at it.

"Is that nice to say, Brent?" Nicole asked.

"It's true," Brent said.

I caught Eli's eye across the table and he smiled. He was laid-back, but he was also deliberately letting people talk the way they wanted in their own house.

"What's your name again?" Nicole looked at me.

"Cray." I piled corn on my plate.

"No, it's not," Sean said. "Your name's Race Car. That's what you said. Race Car."

"Yeah, Race Car," Nicole joined in.

"His name is Race Car," Sean repeated.

Eli shrugged like I had no chance of undoing that.

"Race Car, will you pass the salad?" Brent asked. "Pretty please, Race Car."

I handed him the wooden bowl.

"Thanks, Race Car."

"Do you think we should check with Cray about whether he's okay with being called Race Car?" Stephanie asked.

"Nah." Brent shook his head.

"Are you okay with it?" Sean looked at me expectantly.

So did Brent and Nicole.

This was my first test at Oakcrest, and I knew how to pass. "Yeah, Race Car is fine."

"Race Car." Sean clapped and Nicole grinned. Eli nodded and Stephanie opened her hands in a what-can-you-do way.

A new name was fine. I'd never liked having the same one as Dad and Grandpa.

STEPHANIE LEFT AFTER DINNER AND ELI SHOWED ME how to access program information on the computer. Sean returned Nicole's shampoo and hummed as he cleaned the kitchen. Kate and Nicole watched a Justin Bieber video in the living room and Brent retreated to his room.

Eli talked about how great Stephanie was and said she'd even volunteered to come in at nine so he could get off early because he had a gig. "She's the coolest boss ever," he said.

When it was time to go, Eli walked me down the stairs and Sean called out, "Bye, Race Car."

"Glad you're here, man." Eli opened the door.

"Thanks." I did like him. One more thing that Rayne was right about. I pulled out my phone as I walked and thought about the car I could have had if I'd said yes to Dad.

"How did it go?" Rayne asked when she picked up.

"I think okay."

"How about with Kate?"

"She doesn't like me, and Brent misses Rebecca, but Sean said my name was Race Car and people thought that was funny."

"Race Car?"

"Yeah, long story. I liked Sean and Nicole. Stephanie's great and so is Eli. He seems super laid-back."

"He is," Rayne said. "He brings his guitar and works on songs and everybody likes him, but he's the opposite of Kirsty, who works during the week. Sometimes I wish the two of them were more alike so we had better consistency among staff."

"What are you doing now?" I kicked a stone and hoped she was free.

"Waiting for a Skype call from a friend."

Friend? I wanted to ask, but from the way she said it, I didn't. There was silence between us and then I boldly went ahead. "Let's do something tonight."

"I've got to work at Oakcrest at ten."

"Oh." I was dying to see her. "Let's get together before then."

"I'll call you when I'm done on Skype."

"How long will that be?"

"I don't know," she said quickly. "I've got to go."

"Okay. I'll be at the Edge." I texted Mom that I was hanging out at the coffee shop and would be home later.

I hoped Rayne's friend was a girl, but I had a suspicion he wasn't.

HER FAVORITE PLACE IS WHERE?

I CHECKED THE TIME ON MY PHONE AT THE COFFEE shop. Five minutes since I last looked. I wondered how long I'd have to wait.

I called Jett. "Hey, where are you?"

"At Nora's. Her folks are out tonight."

"Sorry about bowling."

"I warned you," he said sharply.

"I didn't know Rayne and Nora hated each other."

"I told you that."

"No, you didn't."

"Listen, I can't talk. I'm in the middle of something." I could hear Nora's voice in the background as he disconnected.

I'd said I was sorry. Jett could have taken some responsibility. I texted him that, but he didn't respond. I went up to the counter and looked at the cookies. I wasn't hungry, but I needed something to do.

"Can I help you?" a short woman with a gold nose ring asked.

"I'll have one of those." I pointed to a huge white-chocolate-and-macadamia-nut cookie.

I sat down and broke the cookie in half. I wasn't good at waiting, especially when I had no idea how long it would be. I checked my phone again. No texts, no messages, nothing to respond to.

I broke the cookie into smaller pieces. Mom had said I needed a plan for my future, and other than getting a job, I hadn't done anything about it. It felt too big, too overwhelming to know what I was doing instead of going to college, and because of that I didn't want to think about it.

I moved over to the stack of magazines: *Marie Claire*, *Vanity Fair*, *People*, *The Believer*, nothing I wanted to read. I sat back in the chair by the window, the one where I first saw Rayne writing in her notebook. Maybe that's why people wrote in coffee shops. It provided something to do so you didn't sit around looking like a total loser.

AFTER WAITING TWENTY MORE MINUTES, I left. I walked down Division Street past the children's theater, which was advertising a performance of *Mary Poppins*. A couple of empty storefronts displayed costumes and props from the production so they didn't look completely vacant. Downtown was dead, like usual.

I continued to Lincoln Avenue and turned to the river, past the pawnshop. Years ago a bridge for cars had crossed at this spot, but when it got torn down, they put up a pedestrian bridge, and cars stopped coming. The old buildings looked lonely, like they'd been forgotten. Halfway across the bridge, I stopped and guessed how deep the water was. It looked deep enough to jump, but a middle school kid had broken his neck last summer when he dove off the railway bridge upstream—paralyzed for life from one dive.

I leaned over the side and spat in the water. I desperately wanted to see Rayne. Even though I'd known her only a short time, I couldn't get enough of her. She was bold, brave, and bigger in a way than anybody I knew. She didn't care what other people thought and made her own choices and totally understood my decision to not go to college.

At the end of the bridge, I turned around to walk back. Rayne had also confided in me about her mom, and I'd been able to tell her how difficult Dad was. That was big since I didn't normally talk to people that way.

The sun dropped behind a puffy cloud and a light breeze came up. I had to be cautious though, too. There were all kinds of things I didn't know about her, and I wasn't sure how she felt about me. Maybe she just helped out random people and it wasn't a big deal to her. Maybe I was making too much of things.

My phone startled me. I grabbed it out of my pocket. "Hey."

"I'm here at the Edge, Crayster. Where are you?"

"I got tired of waiting there so I'm on the Lincoln Avenue Bridge."

"Don't jump. I'll rescue you."

Rayne's joke wasn't funny. "I'll walk toward the Edge and meet you."

I didn't know what to expect after she'd been talking to her *friend*. Who was he, anyway?

RAYNE SUGGESTED GOING TO HER FAVORITE PLACE, so I followed. "Stephanie texted me," she said. "She liked how you interacted with people."

"I didn't do much."

"You treated everybody with respect. That's what counts. Some new staff get all fake and dramatic. We focus so much on mental ability that we miss all kinds of other abilities."

I thought about that as I hurried to keep up with her. "You like walking."

"Yeah, it gives me time to think." Rayne cut in front of me. "Turn here."

At the end of the short block there were no houses. I looked from side to side. "Where are we going?"

Rayne pointed straight ahead.

"That's the cemetery."

"Yep." She marched along.

I squeezed my hands together. The cemetery was her favorite place? Where did different end and crazy begin?

Rayne strolled through the gates like this was the most natural place to go on a Saturday night. Shadows of gravestones fell on the grass, and my distorted shape bounced awkwardly in front of me.

I hoped she'd tell me something about *her friend*, but she didn't. If I wanted to know, I'd have to ask. "So how did your Skype conversation go?"

"A mix," Rayne said. "It's difficult being so far away."

"Where were you calling?"

"Italy."

"And who were you talking with?"

"Marco."

I paused to give her a chance to say more. She didn't, and we moved deeper into the cemetery.

"Who's he?"

"Marco went to the university here. He graduated and is back in Modena working as a photographer. He wants me to go there."

I wanted to know more, but I also didn't. Of course Rayne hadn't been hanging out with people in high school when she'd had a boyfriend at the university. I felt pretty stupid. Marco was an Italian photographer with a university degree who wanted her to come to Europe. I'd just graduated from high school and didn't know what I was doing. It was no contest: man versus boy.

As we walked along the cemetery path, I tried not to think about him, but that's all I did. I wondered what he looked like, what he sounded like, and what he and Rayne did together. It was driving me crazy and I needed to think about something else, anything else.

So I concentrated on all the dead people and how one day I'd join them. That helped in a weird way. But then I considered what I was doing in the meantime. Giving up a car, not going to college, and hanging out in a graveyard with a girl I really didn't know who already had a boyfriend.

A MESS

WE CONTINUED WITHOUT SAYING ANYTHING AND I focused on the graves: ancient ones with busted-off sides, angel-topped ones that seemed to float above the ground, elaborately detailed ones that looked like miniature castles. All of them saying the same thing—*I'm dead, but please don't forget me.*

The warm breeze carried the scent of cut grass. I slapped a mosquito that had drilled into my arm and brushed another one away from my ear. They didn't seem to be bothering Rayne though she was wearing a T-shirt, too.

Up ahead, an odd shape sat on the ground in front of a grave. "What's that?" I stopped.

"That's Zoran," Rayne said. "When his owner, Mr. Driggs, died, his dog came every day and lay down next to the grave. Then one day he died on this exact spot. Friends had this sculpted, and he was buried here beside his owner." Rayne rubbed the nose of the dog statue. "I don't know how Zoran knew where Mr. Driggs was buried. He might have come out with someone to the cemetery. Maybe he attended the funeral. But people remember seeing him here every time they came to visit no matter what the weather was like."

I bent down and reached out my hand. I pulled it back when I touched the black stone. I'd half expected it to be softer, more like a dog.

Rayne sat down on Mr. Driggs's grave like she was sitting on a chair. "He must have been some man to inspire that kind of love."

I lowered myself to the edge of the grave that faced her. I was nervous knowing there was a body beneath me, so I tried not to think about it as Rayne told me that she, Aaron, and her dad were going to her grandma's the next day. She paused and looked like she realized I hadn't said anything in a while. "What's on your mind?"

Marco was on my mind, but I wasn't ready to hear about him. "Your mom," I said.

"I expected that." Rayne shifted on the stone.

"You don't have to talk about it if you don't want." I picked a tall piece of grass at the base of the stone.

"No, I knew you'd want to know." Rayne exhaled. "I haven't seen her in years. She lives in Peru."

"What happened?"

"She was into exploring different religions." Rayne's voice was soft. "When I was little, she started following this guru."

She paused and crickets chirped as I wrapped my mind around the weird rhyme of *guru* and *Peru.*

"My dad did, too, but he started having doubts when the guru asked them to give up things."

"Like what?"

"First it was money, but later the guru wanted them to sell all their possessions and give the profits to the community."

86

"Did they do that?"

"Yeah, some." Rayne shifted her position.

"Then what happened?"

"The guru decided marriage was an institution of repression and people shouldn't be chained to one partner." Rayne paused like she was deciding how much to tell. "My dad doesn't like to talk about it, but I've done some research on my own. The guru wanted to have sex with all the women and claimed that was the way to enlightenment. That's when my dad dropped out. He wanted my mom to, but she wouldn't, so they got a divorce."

If it were anybody else, I would have doubted the story, but I believed Rayne. "How old were you?"

"Five, and Aaron was one."

"What happened after that?"

"The guru decided to move the community to Peru to be closer to 'a spiritual energy center.' My mom wanted Aaron and me to join her, but Dad went to court to keep us here. He was the one taking care of us, so the judge gave him full custody and we stayed."

"And you haven't seen her since?"

"One time. She came back when I was nine. She didn't act the way I remembered her. She talked like she was reciting a script about the guru and the transformative power of his infinite love. She begged me to come with her to follow the righteous path. That was so unfair, to put me in that position of choosing between her and Dad and Aaron." Rayne sounded sad as she talked, and I imagined her as that scared little kid. "She was angry when I wouldn't go, and after she left, I didn't hear from her for a long time."

"Do you hear from her now?"

"Twice a year. I get a card on my birthday with no gift and I get a color picture of the guru at the beginning of the year. That one goes unopened straight into the trash."

"Wow."

She looked up. "Most people freak when they hear this and want to keep their distance. I won't be shocked if you do, too."

"No." It was the opposite. I was being drawn to her, to her honesty, her courage, her vulnerability. She'd been through something huge, and she trusted me with it, which made me want to know even more. She was so different and that difference pulled me in.

"My life is screwed up." She ran her fingers through her short hair. "I'm a mess."

She was right in front of me—this strange, beautiful, mysterious person. "You're not a mess."

"Yes, I am," she said. "When your mom abandons you, it's hard not to be."

I sat there on the uneven gravestone and imagined being abandoned by my mom. It was impossible. What kind of mom would do that? Hearing Rayne's story made me want to be there for her, to protect her somehow. I wanted to move next to her and put my arm around her, but that didn't feel right, and there was still another person between us.

"And what about Marco?"

Suddenly Rayne stood up. "I've got to be at Oakcrest."

"Wait." I had a ton of questions to ask.

"We can talk about it another time." Rayne rushed off.

I watched her go and pulled out my phone and saw we still had time. I called her but she wouldn't answer. We could have walked together and kept talking. Maybe she was afraid she'd said too much.

I looked around and listened. Branches squeaked and leaves

whispered. I stood up and stared into the dark. Something moved and it seemed like shapes were shifting. I called her again, but she didn't answer. A mosquito bit my neck and I slapped it. Blood smeared on my palm, so I spat on it and wiped it off in the grass. I turned around and felt like I was being watched.

I ran back to the entrance. Near the gate, I tripped and fell. I banged my elbow on the pavement and it throbbed with pain. I was hesitant to look but relieved there wasn't blood. It hurt badly as I held it against my stomach while I made sure my phone wasn't smashed. I searched for what I'd tripped over, but nothing was obvious.

As I walked downtown holding my arm like a sling, I had no clue where to go. I didn't want to go home, and Jett was out with Nora. There was only one person I wanted to see: Rayne. She'd said she'd understand if I wanted to keep my distance, but that was the opposite of what I wanted. I called again, but still nothing.

Ehnnnnn. A horn blared and brakes squealed. I jumped back as an SUV missed me by a few feet.

"Are you trying to get yourself killed, dumb-ass?" the driver yelled.

I stood, stunned. I'd been on my phone and hadn't even looked. I could have been dead in an instant.

I exhaled a deep breath and made a decision. Even as I did, I knew it was bad, but I had to see her.

FIVE MINUTES AFTER TEN, I approached the driveway at Oakcrest and saw Rayne on the couch in front of the window. I should have turned around and gone home. But instead, I climbed the steps and pressed the handle of the door, and it opened. I stepped quietly inside.

Rayne jumped up. "What the hell are you doing?" she whispered.

"I need to know a couple of things."

"Not here, not now."

"Just a couple of questions." I hurried up the stairs holding my elbow and noticed all the bedroom doors were closed.

"You shouldn't be doing this, Cray. What's the matter with your arm?"

"Nothing." I sat down on the couch. "I need to know about Marco."

"You're not supposed to be here."

"Just a few minutes. Tell me about him."

"Marco." Rayne sat down and sighed. "It's complicated."

"What's complicated?"

"I love him, but I'm not moving to Modena to get married. I'm only eighteen, and a mess, but I'm smart enough to know one thing: I'm not ready to be married to him or anybody else."

I was shocked to hear the word *married* but relieved she wasn't doing that. She wasn't going to Italy either, but she'd said the word *love*, that she loved him. I imagined what he looked like: Italian, dark hair, four or five years older than me, probably a stud. I was jealous of someone I'd never met.

"How often do you talk to him?" I asked.

"Shh." Rayne put her finger to her lips.

I couldn't hear anything, but suddenly headlights shone on the window. Rayne's mouth dropped open as she looked out. "It's Stephanie."

I ran to the coat closet. "I'll hide in here."

"Don't be an idiot. She probably already saw you."

I wanted to unlock the patio door and jump off the deck.

Rayne could insist I hadn't been here, that Stephanie had imagined it. Before I could do anything, though, the door opened and Stephanie flew up the stairs.

"What are you doing?" She stood in front of me with her mouth set and her eyes narrowed, completely different from the easygoing person she'd been at dinner.

I considered saying I was talking with Rayne about routines and procedures, but that was an obvious lie. "I had a couple of questions for Rayne."

"It's completely inappropriate for you to be here on a night you're not working." Stephanie stabbed her finger against my chest. "I took a chance hiring you even though Gail was concerned about your maturity. Being here proves her point."

I nodded. Nothing I could say would justify my stupid decision.

She turned toward Rayne. "You know better. You know how we run this house."

Rayne looked like she was about to cry.

"I came back for my phone." Stephanie went into the kitchen and picked it up. "And I find this. It better not ever happen again."

I shifted from one foot to the other.

"One more mistake like this and I'll fire you both." She pointed at me. "Get out of here right now."

I left without saying anything. I'd screwed things up not just for myself, but for Rayne, too.

I wandered around aimlessly and my elbow throbbed. The one person I wanted to talk to was Rayne, and I'd blown it.

When I finally went home, I went straight to my room. I held my bad arm against my chest and lay back on my bed, realizing I'd totally messed up.

BE CAREFUL

A TALL, DARK-HAIRED MAN with a thin mustache and expensive sunglasses walked hand in hand with Rayne through narrow cobblestoned streets. Old buildings jutted out at sharp angles, and I hid behind one as I peeked around to see what they were doing.

Rayne wore her Goodwill bowling shoes, a red skirt, and a white button-down shirt. The man, who was dressed stylishly in black, presented a gift to her as they sat down on a stone bench. Rayne eagerly ripped the paper off and opened the box to reveal a sparkling pair of silver high heels. He bent down and removed one of her bowling shoes, then placed the new shoe on her foot. It fit perfectly and she beamed. He slipped the other one on and she stood up and twirled with delight. He came to her, leaned in, and began to unbutton her shirt. Rayne looked up and smiled and their lips met for a long kiss as he ran his hands all over her. I wanted to hurl a rock and crush his skull, but I was frozen in place.

"Cray, get up." Lansing shook my shoulder.

"Leave me alone." I hadn't finished my nightmare.

"Ten minutes until we leave for church. Dad's asking where you are."

"Tell him I'm not going." I rolled over and my elbow throbbed.

"What?"

"I'm not going."

"I'm not telling him that. C'mon, Cray." Lansing hurried out of the room.

I pulled the pillow over my head and tried to go back to the dream and be braver. I wanted to kill Marco and rescue Rayne.

"Cray, what's the matter?" Mom knocked at the door. "Are you sick?"

"No."

"I'm coming in to check." She opened the door, pulled the pillow away from my head, and put her palm on my forehead. "You don't feel like you have a temperature."

I inhaled her perfume. "I'm not sick."

"Then why aren't you dressed?"

"I'm not going to church today." I pulled away from her.

"Why not?"

"I need to be by myself."

"We go to church every Sunday."

I didn't respond. Doing things the way we always did didn't seem like a good enough reason.

"Everybody will notice if you're not with us and ask where you are."

That didn't seem important either.

"Oh, Cray," she sighed. "Your father is going to be angry."

I pulled the pillow back over my head. I was fed up with Dad's anger being the reason we did things. I was finished with high school and didn't care what he said about the frontal lobes of my brain. I was old enough to make my own decisions.

I heard Mom go downstairs and knew she was on her way to tell him. I sat up in bed and listened to muffled voices in the kitchen. I got up and pulled on shorts and a T-shirt so I wouldn't be in bed when he came in.

"What the hell is going on?" I heard Dad's voice before he got to my room.

"Nothing," I said calmly even though my stomach was churning.

"Get ready for church," he growled.

"I'm not going."

"Listen to me." The tendons in his neck stuck out. "We go to church every Sunday in this house."

"I don't want to today." I took a step back from him.

"I don't care what you want. When you live under our roof, when you eat our food, you follow our rules."

"I'm not a kid." I took another step back. "Besides, you said I needed to pay rent to live here."

"Where is it? I haven't seen any damn rent."

"I haven't gotten paid yet."

"If you're not dressed for church and in the car in three minutes, you'll regret it. Three minutes!"

I sat back on my bed as he stormed out of the room. My head hurt as I remembered last night. I'd really screwed up by going to Oakcrest. I hadn't officially started, and Stephanie was already angry with me.

"Maybe he's sick. Maybe there's something wrong with him," Mom said outside the door.

"He's sick, all right," Dad thundered. "There's definitely something wrong with him."

I lifted my middle finger and waited. I wasn't going anywhere. I heard the front door open and imagined the three of them standing together.

The door slammed shut and the house went quiet. I listened to the BMW start, back up, and drive away.

I bent over and rubbed my forehead. I couldn't get that image of Marco with his hands all over Rayne—and her enjoying it—out of my mind.

After taking a couple of Advil and gobbling down a chocolate-chip granola bar, I called Jett. There was no way I was waiting around for Dad to return. I expected to feel better after standing up to him, but I didn't. I'd jumped off a cliff and was swimming with sharks. I could be chewed up anytime.

"What's up, Cray Man?" Jett answered.

"Nothing," I said. "Can I come over?"

"Sure."

I WENT ACROSS TO THE SHADY SIDE OF THE STREET since it was already hot, and I kept thinking about Rayne. She talked about *different* being good, but then her mom did some-thing hugely different, and it was clear that was bad. Abandoning your own kids was terrible.

Rayne had said she was a mess like she was warning me. But she didn't act like a mess. Compared to most kids our age, she seemed to have her shit together. I was the one who'd messed up last night.

But that nightmare with Marco gnawed away at me, especially since she said she loved him.

Jett was sitting outside on his porch by himself with no Nora in sight.

He lifted up his Coke. "Want something to drink?"

"Sure."

He went into the house and I sat down on the porch swing. I hadn't forgotten about bowling but decided to let it go.

"How well do you know Rayne?" I asked as he handed me a Sprite.

"Why are you obsessed with her?"

"I'm not obsessed. I just want to find out what you know." I held the cold can against my forehead.

"What I told you. How she's smart, how she helped me, how she's got strong opinions about things. But she can be intense. I don't know if she's right for you."

"What do you mean?" I snapped open the Sprite. "That I'm not smart enough for her?"

"I didn't say that."

"What then?" I was sick of him hinting at things.

"She's really different. That's all."

"What's the matter with different? We could use more different around here. I'm sick of everything being the same." I was sounding like Rayne.

"Do what you want." Jett crushed his empty can. "Just be careful."

"What do you mean?"

"Nothing." He shook his head. "Forget it."

I looked directly at him. I wasn't forgetting.

THE CRASH

SUNDAY AFTERNOON, I lounged in a deck chair next to Jett and Nora by her backyard pool.

"Where's Rayne?" she asked.

"At her grandma's."

"That's too bad," she said, but didn't sound convincing.

I closed my eyes against the sun and worried about Rayne being angry. I'd messed up bad. Then I remembered our conversation in the cemetery. I bet not many people knew about Rayne's mom. She had trusted me with something important, but then I'd blown it by forcing the Marco issue.

"Teagan was asking about you," Nora said.

I opened an eye, though I wasn't interested.

"Did you know she's lifeguarding over at Lake Winona?"

"Yeah."

"She looked great at her graduation party yesterday." Nora adjusted her bikini top. "She's totally tan."

"Totally?" Jett asked.

"You know what I mean." She tossed a towel at him.

"I need to cool off." Jett stood up.

Nora got up. She looked hot in her tiny purple bikini. She and Jett dove into the pool and I kept thinking of Rayne and wondered what kind of swimsuit she'd wear. I wished she was with us. But there was no way she'd be doing this. Rayne wouldn't hang out at a pool in the middle of the afternoon and she wouldn't be caught dead at Nora's.

Nora climbed onto Jett's shoulders and they fooled around in the water. She was so obvious, talking about Teagan like that. As if Teagan would be better for me than Rayne just because Nora liked Teagan and was scared of Rayne. Nora wasn't honest. I hadn't noticed that until Rayne pointed it out. Maybe I should be warning Jett about her.

What was I doing anyway? Jett had asked me to come over after our "forget it" exchange because he knew I didn't have anything to do. But everything that Nora said irritated me and reminded me of Rayne.

I had no place to go, though. I wasn't going home with Dad making threats. Rayne wouldn't be back until later. So I pulled a towel over my face and leaned back and tried to ignore the laughing and splashing by imagining being someplace else, some other country far away.

SUNDAY EVENING, when I rang the bell at Oakcrest, nobody answered right away and I hoped Stephanie wasn't inside. Eli had said what a cool boss she was, but I'd seen another side of her. She could be fierce.

A woman with shoulder-length blond hair came to the door. "Oh, hello."

"Hi, I'm Cray. I'm here for orientation."

"I'm Kirsty. I work weekday evenings."

"Nice to meet you." I stood on the step and waited for her to open the door wider or to step back to let me in. She didn't do either, and I worried I'd been fired without Stephanie telling me.

"Am I supposed to be here?"

"Yeah, Stephanie said you'd be coming. Dinner's finished and the kitchen's finally cleaned. I had to have Sean redo the counters three times. He starts telling stories and forgets what he's doing. You have to stay on top of him." Finally she stepped back and I moved inside.

The living room was quiet as I climbed the stairs. "Where's everybody?"

"In their rooms," Kirsty said. "They enjoy their privacy."

On TV, an infomercial for a new-and-improved super juicer promised to restore youthful vigor.

A door opened and Nicole emerged. "Hi, Race Car."

"Hey, Nicole." I moved to the couch.

"What did you call him?" Kirsty turned off the TV.

"He said we could call him Race Car." Nicole sat down.

"I'm sure he didn't," Kirsty said. "I suggest you call him by his proper name."

Nicole looked confused and turned to me.

"Well, umm . . . actually I did." My heel started tapping away.

"You said they could call you Race Car?" Kirsty arched her eyebrows.

"Yeah." That no longer seemed like such a bright idea.

"I don't think that's age appropriate." Kirsty pulled a pair of knitting needles and a ball of gold yarn from a bag. "It's very important that the people who live here conduct themselves in a manner appropriate to their age. They need to call you Cray."

I rubbed my hands together and didn't know what to do. All kinds of things I did probably weren't appropriate for my age.

"I suggest you go to your room, Nicole." Kirsty's needles flew. "Cray and I have some business to discuss."

Nicole stood slowly and shuffled down the hall. The house didn't feel at all like it had at dinner last night.

"So how did you hear about the job here?" She adjusted her needles while she talked.

"Rayne told me about it."

"You know Rayne?" She arched her eyebrows again.

"Yeah."

"She's different," Kirsty pronounced.

That was the worst thing she could have said.

"Have you worked with people with disabilities before?" she asked.

"No, but my cousin has Down syndrome."

"Well, you have to pay attention. You can't be manipulated into doing things for them. Everybody needs to be as independent as possible."

I disliked Kirsty immediately. Her approach was so much more distrustful than Rayne's and Eli's. I sat back on the couch as she elaborated on her techniques of monitoring people and making sure they weren't slacking off.

"Each person does it differently," she said. "Sean does it with his stories and jokes. Nicole does it with her inattentiveness and Kate with her pretend helplessness. Brent's pretty good, but he does things too fast. You've got to watch them."

Kirsty set down her knitting and showed me a bunch of forms on the computer. She went through each one in detail and stressed the importance of documentation "to cover your behind." She didn't seem to enjoy the people in the house and talked about them more negatively than Eli, Rayne, and Stephanie did.

A crash came from the end of the hall.

"What's that?" I turned toward her.

"Probably Brent knocking something over again." Kirsty waved it off.

"Brent, are you okay?" Nicole opened her door.

"What happened?" Sean stepped out.

"Everybody, relax." Kirsty led the way and I followed.

Kate peeked out of her doorway.

"Brent, are you okay?" Kirsty called out.

No answer. Just the *beep, beep* of a Road Runner cartoon on his TV.

"Answer me. Are you okay?"

Nothing.

Kirsty opened the door to Brent thrashing about on the floor. "He's having a seizure. Everybody, get back in your rooms. Help me, Cray."

Brent's fingers locked as his arms flailed back and forth. I was hesitant to move closer as it was one of the scariest things I'd ever seen.

"Clear a space around him," she commanded.

I pulled a chair and a lamp back as Brent kicked strongly. Kirsty knelt down beside him and took off his glasses and set them out of the way. "You'll be okay, big guy."

Brent's eyes rolled back and then closed.

"Help me move him onto his side." She grabbed a pillow and placed it beside his head.

I cautiously got on the other side and we gently rolled Brent over. Drool oozed out of his mouth and pooled onto the pillow. Gurgling noises deep in his throat sounded like he might die.

But Kirsty sat calmly beside him and repeated that he was going to be fine. Gradually the seizure subsided and Brent opened his eyes with a blank look on his face.

"Just a seizure, big guy." She patted him on the shoulder.

Brent nodded.

"Rest a bit." Kirsty brushed Brent's hair back and took a tissue and wiped his mouth.

Brent was pale, but his breathing returned to normal.

"Cray, help me get Brent to his bed. He'll want to sleep after this."

I got behind one of Brent's shoulders while Kirsty took the other and we helped him stand. Together, we guided him slowly to his bed.

"Good job," Kirsty said as he lay back, and it felt like she was saying it to all three of us.

Brent looked dazed, like he'd been in the fight of his life. I didn't want him to think I was staring, so I turned to the TV, where the Road Runner dropped an anvil on Wile E. Coyote. That's probably what a seizure felt like.

Kirsty adjusted the pillow under Brent's head and I turned off the TV. "Rest well," she said. "I'll be down to check on you in a little bit."

I exhaled as we shut the door. "Is it okay to leave him?"

"Yeah, he'll sleep now. He's had these tonic-clonic seizures his whole life, so he knows how to deal with them. The first time you see one is scary, but for Brent, they're part of who he is."

I remembered that Stephanie had mentioned Brent's seizures and said he worked harder than anybody she'd ever met.

"I've got to call the nurse to tell her what happened," Kirsty said. "She wants us to monitor things with the medication change."

"Is there anything else I can do?"

"No, feel free to go. Brent will be fine and we covered the orientation basics. Sorry we had so much drama for you."

"No problem." I walked down the steps and kept picturing Brent's seizure. At least it didn't involve blood. Still, this job was becoming more than I expected.

I GOT OUT MY PHONE AND CALLED RAYNE. "Are you home?"

"Just back." I couldn't tell from her tone how angry she was.

"Brent had a seizure," I said quickly.

"Oh no, I was worried about those new meds."

"He's doing okay now. Resting. Kirsty handled everything. Do you want to get together?"

"No."

"Why not?"

"I need some time," she said coolly, almost like someone I didn't know.

"I'm sorry about last night. I shouldn't have done that."

She didn't respond and I feared I'd lost the connection. "What's the matter?"

"I can't explain."

"C'mon, Rayne," I pleaded. "You owe me an explanation."

"No, I don't. I don't owe you anything." The phone went dead.

I phoned back, but she wouldn't answer. "Call me!" I shouted at her voice mail.

What the hell was going on? I felt like an anvil had dropped on my head, too. I'd said I was sorry and needed to talk. Rayne was the one person I was hanging on to, and she'd just let go. I thought she was someone who had things together. Maybe she didn't.

Maybe she was as messed up as she said.

SOME SPACE

I SHOVED MY PHONE IN MY POCKET AND KEPT WALKING. I had no place to go. Home was out, with Dad's warning of *You'll regret it* echoing in my head. What would he do? Ground me or give me a time-out like he did when I was little?

When I called Rayne again, she wouldn't answer. I thought maybe I should go over to her place and bang on the door. But even as I considered it, I knew I wouldn't. I was afraid nobody would answer and I'd have to slink away.

I thought about buying some chocolate or flowers. That's what guys did in movies when they were trying to get the girl back. But that seemed stupid. I didn't know if Rayne even liked chocolate or flowers, and she hadn't been mine in the first place.

I ended up at the park. I guessed there was about an hour of light left and I hoped it would finally start to cool off. I sat down on a bench and contemplated leaving town. But I didn't have a car and I didn't know where to go. Other than that, it was a brilliant idea.

On the basketball court, two boys went back and forth in a

tight game. The younger one gave up about a foot in height but he played hard and beat the taller guy to every loose ball.

I remembered how much I'd loved hoops at that age. It was a way to get out of the house, to get away from Dad, and to lose myself in the game. As I got older, bad coaches sucked the fun out of it and I lost confidence. By the time I made varsity as a senior, I sat on the bench and watched Jett win games for us.

I spotted a basketball beside the court and walked down. "Can I use it?"

"Yeah," the younger one said as sweat glistened on his dark skin.

I went down to the other end and banked shots off the board and thought about Rayne. I'd screwed up and didn't know what to do. I wanted to work it out, but she wasn't giving me a chance.

At the far hoop, the young guy made a tough reverse layup for the win. His friend left on his bike and he came down to get his ball. I passed it to him at the three-point line and he launched a shot that dropped through. I passed the ball back and he swished another one. When he finally missed, he passed the ball to me to shoot.

I hit a fadeaway from the baseline. He fired me a bounce pass and I made two more before I missed and gave it back to him. It felt surprisingly good to be back on the court. It was still a place to go when things went bad.

We took turns shooting to the rhythm of the bouncing ball. Then it hit me. I couldn't chase Rayne. I had to wait and give her some space until she was ready to talk. I couldn't think only about what I wanted. I had to think about what she needed, too.

Giving her space would be hard, because I wanted to sort things out as soon as possible. I drained a free throw and made a resolution to myself: I wasn't talking to her until she talked to me first.

The young kid made five three-pointers in a row and I kept feeding him.

"You've got a nice game."

"Thanks." He rattled another one home.

I CALLED JETT AND HE PICKED UP ON THE FIRST RING.
"What're you doing?"

"Hanging out at home," he said.

"With Nora?"

"No, she's at her aunt's cat's birthday party."

"What?"

"That was my reaction. Her aunt doesn't have any kids and claims her cat is as much a part of the family as any two-legged creature. She says he deserves the same type of birthday cele-bration as everybody else."

"That's crazy. Does he get cake?"

"No cake but some kind of cat treat. Nora asked me to go, but I drew the line at a party for a cat. Come on over."

"Okay." I considered trying Rayne once more and studied her name on my Favorites list, but I remembered my resolution.

Still, that was a hard call not to make.

AT JETT'S WE PLAYED *CALL OF DUTY*, watched Comedy Central, and ate mini Snickers. After everything that had happened, it was good to hang out.

Just because I'd resolved not to call Rayne didn't mean I could stop thinking about her. "What did you mean when you told me to be careful with Rayne?"

"Look out for yourself," he said.

"Why?"

"She's got a boyfriend. Some Italian guy."

"Yeah, Marco." I tried to sound cool with it. "He's back in Italy."

Jett unwrapped another Snickers and shoved it in his mouth. "She's really into him."

"I know. We've discussed it."

Jett's phone buzzed and he reached over to grab it. "Hey, how's Birthday Cat?"

I flipped through TV channels while they talked but then Jett handed me the phone. "Nora wants to talk to you."

"Yeah." I held it cautiously like it might blow up.

"I can tell you're not interested in Teagan, but I saw Kenna at the mall and she asked what you were doing this summer."

"Yeah."

"Cray, she wants you to ask her out again. She likes you."

"Kenna likes everybody. That's why she was class president."

"That's mean. What's the matter with you? I'm telling you she's into you."

I passed the phone back to Jett. I didn't trust her. She was trying to sabotage Rayne and me, and I didn't need help with that. I was doing enough to mess things up. I picked up the remote and finally found something to watch, *lucha libre*, Mexican wrestling.

When Jett finished, he grabbed the last Snickers. I waited for him to say what was happening, but he didn't.

"Is Nora coming over?"

"No, she's got a meeting at work tomorrow that she's getting ready for."

"Can I stay over again?"

"Yeah, it's cool with my folks."

"Thanks." I texted Mom and then turned off my phone as Jett and I watched tag teams of three wearing brightly colored masks leap off the ropes and fly around the ring.

"Nora's trying to help," he said. "It would be fun to do stuff together. That's not happening with Rayne."

"I know. I've got to figure this out for myself."

THE NEXT MORNING, Jett dropped me off at the Edge on his way to camp. I stared at Rayne's spot in the window from outside, but it was empty. *Please let me see her*, I pleaded as I walked in and smelled coffee. *Please*.

But she wasn't there.

I ordered a cappuccino and poured sugar in. The golden crystals sank slowly into the froth and I felt like I was being pulled down, too. A couple of days ago, I'd been so excited. Now I was full of doubt. I took out my phone and set it on the table. I was dying to call but remembered my resolution. It was hard to hang on to that.

Someone had left a Sharpie on the table and I picked it up and wrote our names side by side on a napkin.

Cray Rayne

We both had *ray* in common and that felt like a sign. Rayne had been a ray of light for me, the way she'd lit up my summer. She'd also been a ray of hope when she got me the Oakcrest job.

But there was also another kind of ray, a stingray. I typed *stingray* into my phone for a definition: *Any of various rays having a whip-like tail and venomous spines capable of inflicting serious bodily injury.*

Serious bodily injury?

The door opened and I crumpled the napkin, but it wasn't Rayne. Instead Teagan zoomed over. "Hey, Cray."

"Hi." Nora was right. Teagan was tan. So tan so fast that it couldn't all have been from the sun. She must have been spending time in tanning beds or spraying it on. Maybe she *was* totally tan.

"I missed you at my graduation party," she said.

"Sorry, I had to work." I didn't feel like attending graduation parties since I wasn't having one of my own, but I was sorry to miss out on the cash.

"It was fun!" Teagan grinned, and her white teeth stood out against her tan skin. "But I'm still not sure where I'm going. I'm stuck on that stupid waiting list at Carleton, and not knowing is terrible." She reached into her purse and pulled out a piece of paper. "I've got to pick up muffins for our lifeguard meeting." She grabbed the Sharpie from me and wrote her number. "Call me sometime."

"Okay." I wasn't planning to and didn't want to be talking to Teagan if Rayne came in.

My phone buzzed and I jumped with excitement. But then I saw it was Mom. "Yeah."

"Where are you?"

"At the coffee shop." I waved to Teagan as she left.

"Doing what?"

"Ah, drinking coffee." I slurped some.

"Don't get smart with me," she said. "How did it go at Jett's?"

"Fine."

"Listen, Cray, I spoke with your father this morning. We both want you to sleep here tonight."

"Did he say that?" I folded Teagan's number into smaller and smaller pieces.

"He wants you back. Staying away isn't solving anything."

"Being at home wasn't either."

"That's no way to talk. We expect you here tonight. Can you promise that?"

"No, I can't. I'm staying at Jett's."

I WAITED OVER AN HOUR FOR RAYNE, but she never showed. I even bought a wheat-free banana-nut muffin and set it on the table hoping it would act as a magnet. It didn't, so I ate it, and it tasted better than I expected.

I bought a replacement muffin, put it in a paper bag, and set off across the river. I replayed our last conversation as I moved past the dilapidated buildings and brick warehouses. I hadn't meant to get Rayne chewed out by Stephanie, and I'd apologized.

When I got to her building, the metal door was locked, so I knocked and waited for an answer. Nobody came and I had to slink away like I'd feared.

I crossed the street and looked up, but there were no windows visible. I walked down the uneven cobblestones to find a better spot, but a tall brick wall blocked my view. I took a left at the next corner, but I still couldn't see in because of the wall. Coming down had been a stupid idea.

I followed the street, which was full of potholes, to the edge of a millstream. It dead-ended, but upstream about thirty yards was a rusted bridge. A path snaked along the bank to the bridge, and I followed it. I looked up at the top of Rayne's building. Three big windows with panes of clouded glass faced my way. It was impossible to see inside, but I had the feeling that she was there. Maybe watching me.

I crossed the bridge and moved cautiously down a broken sidewalk on the other side. Rayne's building went all the way to the stream, and I hoped I could get a clearer view.

A scrawny orange cat darted in front of me and hissed. I stopped and looked around. Some buildings had padlocked doors, but many seemed like they'd been abandoned for years. I found some crumbling concrete steps and climbed down. In front of me, Rayne's building towered above the stream where water spilled over a small dam.

I scanned the building. Two floors had the clouded windows, but the top floor had big windows of clear glass. A shape floated across the room, but I might have been imagining things. I stood and watched the windows, hoping to see her.

"What the hell are you doing?" a voice rasped. I jumped and turned around. A short guy with a stubby beard and a dirty base-ball hat waved a metal pipe in front of my face like a sword.

"Nothing. Nothing. I was just looking around."

"For what?" he asked.

"I don't know." To say *Rayne* would have sounded like I was stalking her.

"No strangers," the old guy barked.

"Okay." I held up my hands like I was under arrest as I climbed the steps. I kept an eye on him so he wouldn't take a swing at me with the pipe.

I didn't know where he had come from, but he scared me. He kept the pipe extended as I got away. At the road I turned and crossed the bridge. I stopped to look back at Rayne's building. I felt uneasy, though, like I was doing something wrong. I checked upstream, where the old man was still watching me.

"No strangers." He shook the pipe like some psycho killer.

As I hurried along the road, I had my first good idea of the day. I circled back to the metal door of Rayne's building and set down the muffin bag. I looked around to make sure the crazy guy wasn't following me and then moved the bag closer to the door. It wasn't chocolate or flowers, but it was better. It was something specifically for her. I hoped she'd get it and know who it was from.

COMPLICATED

JUST BEFORE NOON, I walked up the driveway of our house. Nobody would be there, but I still checked around to make sure. I unlocked the back door and felt like I was sneaking into somebody else's place. "Hey," I called.

Nobody answered. Nothing moved. But an uneasy feeling gnawed at me as I thought about Dad's warning. I couldn't guess what he'd come up with. And that itself put me on edge.

My stinky shirt indicated I needed clean clothes as I entered the living room, which felt more like a museum than a room where people lived. No stray glasses or coffee mugs were out. Everything was perfect and in its proper place. I felt uncomfortable, like I didn't belong.

I looked up at the yellow jaguar mask on the wall and remembered how Dad had made me negotiate in Spanish for it when we were in Mexico for spring break. On the other wall, a black-and-white picture of the four of us from last year stared back. Mom had insisted we dress up and go into a studio, and she debated the pros and cons of different shots before selecting one. I looked goofy in it, but Mom loved it because everyone was smiling. It was weird to display a big picture of ourselves in our own home, but that was Mom's image of us, what she desperately wanted to believe.

I charged my phone in my room and shoved clean boxers, T-shirts, and shorts into my backpack. In my bathroom, I shaved, took off my clothes, and got in the shower. I stood under the hot water and thought about Rayne confiding in me and then cutting me off.

As I dressed, I tried to figure out where to go for the afternoon. Jett was working. The coffee shop reminded me too much of Rayne. Nothing good popped into my mind as I gathered up my toothbrush, toothpaste, body spray, phone, and charger.

I closed the back door with a *thunk* and slung my backpack over my shoulder. I was leaving home with no place to go. Pretty pathetic.

I STOPPED FOR PIZZA.

"Did you find a job?" Sam asked.

"Yeah, I'm working nights with adults with developmental disabilities."

"Good for you."

"I'm still looking for another job during the day."

"Sorry, I don't have an opening," she said.

As I ate my slices, I remembered Dad demanding I get another job. I hadn't done anything on that. I wished I had so I'd have a place to go.

My phone buzzed and I grabbed it. The name on the screen filled me with excitement: *Rayne.* "Yeah." I attempted to sound calm.

"Sorry for being a bitch last night."

"You weren't a bitch." An old woman at the next booth glared at me, so I grabbed my plate and moved outside.

"I need my Oakcrest job, Cray. I can't jeopardize it."

"I know. I need mine, too." I sat on the bench in front of Sam's. "I'm sorry. What I did was stupid. I should have listened to you."

"It can't happen again," Rayne said.

"I know. It won't."

Then Rayne told me all about her visit to her grandma's and why she'd been in a bad mood. "We got out old pictures and there were a couple of my mom and dad together. Grandma said some mean things about my mom, and then Dad defended her even though it's pretty indefensible. It's like, it's okay if we criticize her, but we don't want other people to do it. After all, she's the only mom I've got no matter what she's done."

As she talked, I realized how much I'd missed her—her voice, her energy, her self.

"Thank you," she said.

"For what?" I ate my last bite of pizza.

"For the banana-walnut muffin you left at the door."

"How'd you know it was me?"

"Because you're sweet," she said. "And because Otto told me."

"Who's Otto?"

"A friend who stays in one of the warehouses."

"The old guy?"

"He's not that old. He's an Iraq War vet who keeps an eye on things down here. He said you seemed strange and were scoping out our building."

"*I* seemed strange? He shoved a metal pipe in my face."

"He takes his job seriously. He was suspicious, but when he saw you'd left a muffin, he thought it might be okay."

"Is it okay?" I asked.

"Is what okay?"

"Us. Back to the way things were."

"Yeah."

"Good." That's what I wanted to hear.

"I talked to Stephanie this morning. She's giving us another chance," Rayne said.

"Did she tell Gail about it?"

"No. It would prove Gail right about not wanting to hire you. Stephanie expects professionalism. You have to promise that."

"I do."

"She asked me to orientate you to the night position," Rayne said. "Can you come in at ten tomorrow night?"

"Sure."

"She's waiting for some paperwork, but she wants you to start as soon as it's approved."

"Great. I need to start making some money."

"What are you doing now?" Rayne asked.

"Nothing. Sitting downtown on a bench."

"Meet me by the fountain outside the art building."

"When?"

"Right now."

"I'm on my way."

I was pumped. The resolution had worked. I'd given Rayne space and she'd come back. I was excited to see her, but things were swinging around wildly.

Knowing Rayne was complicated.

RAYNE LOUNGED AGAINST THE WALL IN FRONT OF THE fountain reading a book. She wore an orange dress, a green scarf, and her bowling shoes.

She turned her head. "Cray." She jumped off the wall and ran to me. She held out her arms like a bird about to fly. I dropped my pack and wrapped her up in a big hug and felt her body against mine.

"You look good."

She pulled back to examine me. "So do you." It seemed like forever since I'd seen her. Jett had warned me to be careful with Rayne. I'd spent my whole life being careful, and what had it gotten me? I was ready to take a risk.

"I love my new shoes." She lifted one and then the other and did a little dance holding the book over her head. Other people eating lunch turned to watch.

"What are you reading?"

"Mary Oliver." She showed me a cover with a woman with dark hair looking to the side, away from the camera. "Murph said I'd like her and I do."

"Cool." I picked up my pack, and when I turned around Rayne was holding out a package.

"For you," she said. "Homemade banana bread with rice flour. Try it and tell me what you think."

I picked out a piece and took a bite. "It's good."

"I'm glad." She took some tortilla chips and an apple out of a paper bag. "Do you want to share my lunch?"

"I just had pizza." I took another bite of banana bread and chewed it slowly.

"What's in your pack?"

I explained about the clothes and Dad and the warning and

Rayne listened—not just pretend listening, but real listening. Her listening was one of the things I liked best about her. It made it easy to tell her things I didn't tell anybody else. Forget careful—this was exactly what I needed.

"So you don't have any plans for dinner?" she asked.

"No."

"Why don't you eat with us? You can meet my dad and brother."

"Okay." I was thrilled to have someplace to go since I was avoiding home. But meeting Rayne's family felt like a whole new level.

AFTER RAYNE WENT BACK TO WORK, I got a call.

"Cray, this is Stephanie. I need you to come by the office today. What time works for you?"

"I'm free now."

"Come down as soon as you can."

I wondered if Rayne was wrong about orientation. Maybe Stephanie was letting her stay but firing me. I picked up my pack and threw it over my shoulder. I absolutely needed to keep my job since I didn't have anything else.

When I got to the office, the first person I saw was Gail, the program director. "Hi." I tried to sound cheerful.

"Hello," she said flatly. "I'll tell Stephanie you're here."

I sat down and worried that Gail had ordered me fired. She'd never wanted me in the first place.

Stephanie walked out looking serious. "Come in, Cray."

I followed her and prayed I'd keep my job.

She closed the door as I sat in front of her desk, which was tidy with pictures of her husband and grown-up sons.

"Rayne assures me that you recognize the severity of your mistake, but I need to hear it from you."

"I definitely do." I attempted to look remorseful. "It will never happen again."

"Good." She turned to a picture of her sons with their arms around each other. "I've parented teen boys, so I believe in second chances. But if something like this happens again, you'll be terminated."

"It won't."

"Make sure." She put on a pair of silver-framed glasses and looked at her computer. "Gail wants to see you now. She's had a complaint."

"About something else?"

She nodded. I got up and walked out in a daze. I couldn't figure out what else I'd done wrong.

Gail pointed at a chair when I entered. "Sit down."

She might be the one to fire me.

"I understand that you've been encouraging behavior that isn't appropriate." She cleared her throat.

"What?"

"Kirsty said you asked people at Oakcrest to call you—" She paused and looked down. "Race Car?"

"I didn't ask that. It was a joke. I was joking with Sean."

She studied her paper. "Kirsty says this does not display the proper level of respect and is not age appropriate."

I squeezed my hands together and wondered at what age it would be appropriate to call someone Race Car.

Gail took off her glasses. "We expect our staff to be professional at all times. We need people to call you by your correct name. Is that understood?"

"Yeah." I attempted to hide my frustration. I hadn't asked anyone to call me Race Car, and Stephanie had been there and hadn't objected. I didn't say that, though, because that would get her in trouble. Figuring out how things worked at Oakcrest was impossible.

She rambled on about professionalism and best practices, but I was furious. Kirsty had already told me how she felt. She didn't need to go behind my back to Gail.

I thought things had gone well when we'd worked together and Brent had his seizure, but then she'd complained about me. I'd worked with her once and she'd turned me in. She was somebody I needed to watch out for.

THE CALL

WHEN I GOT TO RAYNE'S BUILDING, I called like she'd told me to and she came right down.

"Welcome." She wore flip-flops and a green apron that said KISS THE COOK over a violet sundress.

"Are you the cook?" I asked.

"I am." She smiled and her eyes sparkled.

I leaned forward and kissed her on the cheek, but she pulled back.

"For the cook," I said. "Following directions."

"You like to follow directions, don't you?"

"Sometimes. Depends on who's giving them." I wanted to kiss her again, this time on the lips.

"Wouldn't you rather not have directions and find your own way?"

"I don't know. Not if I was trying to get someplace." Talking to Rayne could be confusing, like solving a riddle. I followed her up the stairs as her dress swished back and forth.

"We're the only ones on the third floor," she said. "Some other people live on second, and there's a couple who live behind the woodworking shop on first."

"No elevator?"

"There's a freight one in the back, but it's unreliable. When it breaks, you have to wait until someone comes to fix it."

Getting stuck in an elevator with her sounded exciting, and as she climbed, I admired her legs. Going up and down stairs and walking everywhere must be how she stayed in such good shape.

"You can leave your shoes here." Rayne slipped off her flip-flops at the third-floor landing.

I untied my Nikes and set down my pack. She opened a big wooden door and the smell of food made me hungry. Inside was a long hallway with timber beams and high ceilings.

"This used to be a box factory. They made wooden boxes here originally and then switched to cardboard," Rayne said.

I touched the reddish-brown brick wall. Nobody I knew lived in a place like this. I wondered what Rayne's dad was like if he chose to live around people like the crazy guy who'd threatened me.

At the end of the hall, Rayne turned and a huge room with shiny wooden floors opened up as the evening sun poured in.

"Cray's here," Rayne announced.

A man with light curly hair starting to go gray spun around from his computer and got up.

"Hello." He walked across the room in his bare feet and I was struck by how tall he was. He was over six foot four. Rayne must have gotten her height from him. "I'm Gordon." He held out his hand.

"Hi." I clasped his firm grip and looked into his blue eyes, which didn't look at all like Rayne's.

"How about a glass of iced sun tea with fresh mint?" he asked.

"Okay." This didn't seem like a Coke or Sprite place.

He nodded to Rayne, who put ice cubes into a blue glass. Behind him, the windows let in so much light that it seemed like I could walk out into the sky.

He led me over to the other wall, where things were pulled back from another window and scaffolding was up. "Rayne's putting new glass in here."

I noticed three clear panes of glass in the top row. "That's a big job."

"There are thirty-six pieces of glass in each window." Rayne handed me my tea. "It takes an hour to chip out the old pane, apply new caulk, and install a clear piece."

Gordon went over to the stove to check on a pan.

"We did the west windows first because the sunsets are spectacular." Rayne raised her glass to me in a toast and we clinked.

At the clear window, I surveyed the stream and the cement steps where Otto had threatened me. I took a sip of tea and it tasted better than I expected as I stared across the valley to the bluffs on the other side.

"These long views are supposed to help your eyes relax." Rayne stood close to me.

A couple of skateboards decorated with skulls and flames leaned against the wall. "Is Aaron around?"

"He's on his way. We'll eat when he gets here."

I took another sip as the sun ducked behind a cloud. "Kirsty complained about me to Gail."

"I heard that from Stephanie. That's Kirsty. She does that kind of thing to keep people off-balance. It's a power thing. She's scared of you."

"Scared of me. Why?"

"People at Oakcrest like you. They don't like her. She's got to do something to make you feel uneasy."

"If nobody likes her, why's she at Oakcrest?"

"Didn't I tell you? Kirsty is Gail's sister-in-law. Gail makes sure she keeps her job."

"Oh." I kept looking out the window at the long view. It wasn't working, though, since I still felt nervous.

"You know, Cray, you question yourself a lot."

"I do?"

"See, that's a question."

"Really?"

"That's another one." Rayne laughed.

"Yeah." I turned to her. "I hate being so uncertain about the fall. Everything's always been laid out for me, but now it's not."

"Don't worry." Rayne put her hand on my shoulder. "You'll find it."

WHEN AARON GOT BACK, the four of us sat down to eat at an old table as the sun descended in a burst of orange. Aaron, who was fourteen, seemed kind of shy, but when Rayne asked him questions about skating, he described a new trick he was working on in detail. Aaron had dark hair and brown eyes like Rayne. The two of them must have gotten that from their mom. I wanted to see a picture of her but didn't dare ask.

"How do you like the eggplant, Cray?" Gordon asked.

"It's good."

"That and the tomatoes, peppers, and cucumbers in the salad are from our community garden plot."

Rayne passed me a basket of bread.

"It can use a good watering tomorrow if it doesn't rain tonight," Gordon said.

While I ate, I listened to the three of them discuss how things were growing. Rayne had told Gordon I wasn't going to college in the fall, and I appreciated how he didn't quiz me the way most adults would. He seemed about Dad's age, but he didn't act like him. He was much more relaxed and didn't need to dominate the conversation.

As we were eating caramel ice cream with strawberries, Rayne turned to me. "I told my dad about what happened with you at home. I hope that was okay."

"Yeah." I was surprised.

"Dad, can Cray crash here if he needs to?"

I couldn't believe she was asking.

"No." Gordon shook his head.

"Why not?" Rayne asked.

It was strange to hear them talking about me, and I was embarrassed in front of Aaron, who didn't have any idea what it was about.

"Cray should talk to his dad." Gordon set down his spoon. "He can work this out. When you have a chance to work something out, you need to try."

"But Cray's dad is being unfair," Rayne protested.

"Cray can still make it work."

I sat silently. I hadn't asked to stay. I hadn't thought of it, especially since Rayne would be working at Oakcrest, and it would be too weird to stay here without her. But when Gordon said no, I was still disappointed. I watched the lines in his face and tried to figure him out.

He wasn't like any dad I knew. But then he wasn't a usual dad. With Rayne and Aaron, he'd had to be both mom and dad after his wife split to follow her guru. That had to be really difficult.

AFTER DINNER, Rayne and I were standing outside on the loading dock when her phone rang. She pulled it out and looked at the screen.

"It's Marco. I've got to take this."

She walked away and I overheard her telling him she was with me. She laughed and I wondered what joke he'd made. What terrible timing. Marco was like a ghost hovering over us.

After a few minutes, Rayne came back smiling. "You won't believe it. I can't believe it. Marco's coming. He says he's desperate to see me and can't stay away. He just finished getting his tickets. He'll be here Wednesday."

"No way. This Wednesday?"

"Yes, can you believe it?"

"No." Of course I couldn't.

"He switched some things at work so he can stay for a week. I'm so excited I can't stand it."

I didn't know what to say. All kinds of things could happen in a week.

"I've been telling Marco about you and he's eager to meet you." Rayne kept grinning.

As if that's what I wanted.

GAP LIFE

AFTER I WALKED RAYNE TO OAKCREST, I called Jett. "Is it okay if I stay over again tonight?"

"Ah, just a minute."

I heard a voice in the background. His folks were fine with it, so I knew it wasn't them he was checking with.

"Okay," he said, "come over in half an hour."

"Sure." It had to be Nora.

I went down to the river and thought about Marco coming. I shifted my pack from one shoulder to the other. I was sick of carrying it around like a kid pretending to run away going nowhere.

I considered what Gordon had said. Maybe I should go back and try to deal with Dad. But I couldn't face that and I'd already told Mom I was staying at Jett's. I sat down on a park bench. If anybody saw me, they'd think I was homeless and had no place to go. They'd be right.

I checked my phone and saw I still had twelve minutes to kill. After being warned by Stephanie about professionalism, it didn't feel safe to even call Rayne at work. I wasn't eager to hear more about Marco anyway. I remembered the easy way she and Aaron talked at dinner and chose someone I didn't often call.

"Yeah."

"Hey, Lansing."

"What do you want?"

"Nothing. I'm just saying hi."

"Why aren't you here?" he asked.

"I need a break. How are things?"

"Okay."

Silence hung between us. Lansing and I were so different that we didn't have many regular conversations. Usually we were giving or getting information or ignoring each other.

"They talk about you," he said.

"Who?"

"Mom and Dad. They miss you."

"Yeah, what about you?"

"Nah, they don't talk much about me."

"No, I mean do you miss me?"

"A little," Lansing said. "They've been on me more lately with you gone. When you're here, you take the heat."

"I'm working some things out."

"Like what?"

"What I want, what I'm doing, how I'm dealing with them." I paused. "Do you remember when we went to that shop in Tulum when we were in Mexico?"

"Yeah, I loved that town."

"Me too, but remember how Dad made me do the negotiating for him in Spanish when he wanted that jaguar mask? He kept forcing the shop owner to lower the price by saying what was wrong with it and pretending to walk out." I got up and paced back and forth in front of the bench. "That was embarrassing. Dad could easily have paid what the guy was asking, but instead, he kept driving the price down like it was a game he had to win. I hated being involved in that."

"I didn't like that, either," Lansing said.

"He's doing that with me on St. Luke's. He's trying to force me to accept a deal I don't want."

"But you want to go to college, right?"

"Yeah, but I'm not sure how."

"Okay. I've got to go, Mom's yelling something. See you soon."

I picked up my pack, surprised that Lansing actually seemed to understand some of what I was dealing with. Part of why I'd left was so they could see what it was like without me. It wouldn't be a big deal to be at home for the summer if I were going to college in the fall. But because I wasn't, I felt I had to get started with my life. I needed to figure out my gap year.

AT JETT'S, he and Nora were wrapped around each other on the couch and I was irritated to see her since I'd waited the extra time.

"What did you do tonight, Cray?" she asked.

"I was over at Rayne's." I sat down in the chair across from them.

"Interesting." Nora brushed her hair back.

The way she said *interesting* pissed me off. "What do you mean by that?"

"She already has a serious boyfriend."

I didn't need her reminding me. "What business is it of yours?" I was sick of her interfering.

"Be careful," she said.

"I can make my own decisions." I raised my voice and stood up. She was using the same words Jett had. "What do you even know about Rayne?"

"Hey." Jett got in front of me to try to calm me down.

"What are you saying?" I pushed Jett's hand out of the way.

"Whoa, take it easy," she said.

"What do you mean about Rayne?"

"She can be rough on guys. That's all."

With everything that had happened, I felt ready to explode. Rayne was right. Nora was a manipulating liar. I was about to yell at her, but Jett put his arm on my shoulder and pointed upstairs, where his folks and sisters were.

"What about you, Nora?" I asked. "How do you treat people?"

"What's that supposed to mean?"

"Just that." I was so angry I felt like shoving Jett into her, but I resisted.

"Look in the mirror before you say anything about Rayne."

"I know you're not going to college like the rest of us," she said. "But you don't have to be such a dick about it."

"Shut up!" I turned and stormed out. I wasn't taking that shit from her. I was furious at Jett, too. He'd promised not to tell anybody about me not going.

Outside, I kicked a stop sign and listened to it rattle. I couldn't go home. I'd told Mom and Lansing I wouldn't be there, and to show up now would feel like a defeat. Dad would look at it that way, and I wasn't giving him that.

I WALKED DOWN TO THE UNIVERSITY, past the fountain where Rayne and I'd hung out. I'd had lunch and dinner with her, but now her boyfriend was coming and I was thoroughly confused. I wished I could go to Oakcrest and tell her what had happened with Nora, but that wasn't an option.

Out of desperation, I checked a door of the social sciences building, but it was locked. The next one was, too. But then I found one in back that opened and decided it wasn't breaking in if a university door was unlocked. I opened it quietly and looked down the hall. Nobody in sight. I took a few steps pressed against the wall to make sure it was clear and tiptoed softly down the hallway, checking classroom doors: locked, locked, locked. I heard a noise and jumped, but it was only a fan kicking on.

After a dozen doors, I found one that opened. I stepped into a lecture hall with tiered seating. Down in front was a carpeted area with a podium. That was where teachers lectured to university students, the type of student I wouldn't be. At that moment, I wished I was going to college instead of sneaking around one. My life would be a whole lot easier, and on top of that, I'd have a car.

I waited for a security guard to enter and escort me out, but nobody did. Finally, I took a couple of T-shirts out of my pack and set them on the floor as a pillow. I stretched out on the carpet, which was hard and smelled dirty, and tried not to think about it. I rolled around, experimenting with different positions, desperate to find something that was bearable.

I'd told people I was taking a gap year, but I wasn't going to college a year from the fall. Nobody was paying my way as a star athlete like Jett. I wasn't super smart like Rayne. My gap year could become two years and then three and then four. I didn't see a way I could earn enough money to pay for college on my own. My gap year could turn into my gap life.

FLEXIBILITY

WHEN I WOKE UP, the red numbers of the clock flashed 6:01. I sat up and rolled my head. My neck, shoulders, and back all hurt from the hard floor.

I shoved my shirts into my pack. Nobody would use this room so early, but I didn't want a security guard catching me and asking questions.

Outside, I wanted to phone Rayne, but it was too early, so I considered calling Jett to tell him how pissed I was. He'd betrayed me by telling Nora I wasn't going to college in the fall when he'd promised not to. We'd had arguments before, but nothing like this.

At the Edge, I drank a large coffee at the table by the window, Rayne's table. Maybe because I kept obsessing about her, I wished I had a notebook and a pen to write down some things. So much had changed so quickly that I didn't know what to think.

I checked the time and debated how early was too early to call. They had wheat-free muffins, so I bought two and set them on a plate in the middle of the table. I waited all the way until quarter to seven before finally giving in.

"Rayne, are you up?"

"Yeah, barely."

"I'm at the Edge and I've got something for you. Can you meet me here?"

"I'm getting in the shower. I'll be there in half an hour."

That's what I needed. No hesitation. I got myself more coffee, ate a gooey cinnamon roll, and pictured Rayne in the shower. Then I started to worry that I'd made it sound too dramatic. A muffin wasn't much, even if it was wheat-free.

SHE APPEARED LOOKING SHARP IN BLACK CAPRIS AND a flowing leopard-print top. Her hair was still damp from the shower and her face glowed.

"For you." I pointed to the muffin on the plate.

"What kind?"

"Cranberry-maple-pecan, wheat-free."

"My favorite. You're having one, too?"

"Yeah." I took a bite. It wasn't as good as the cinnamon roll, but I didn't need to mention that. Instead, I told her about the argument at Jett's house. I left out the part about Nora saying Rayne was rough on guys, but I made it clear I'd stood up for her.

Rayne leaned forward and touched my hand. "I don't want to have anything to do with her. She's toxic, and if Jett wants to be with her, I'm not seeing him, either."

"I know." I thought she'd be angry, but instead she was calm. I knew she expected me to choose, too. I was done with Nora, but I couldn't give up on Jett.

I picked out a pecan from my muffin and told Rayne about sleeping on the floor of the classroom.

"You're flexible, Cray. That's one of the things I like about you."

One of the things. That meant there were others.

We talked about dinner at her house and her dad and Aaron and then the conversation shifted to Marco.

"It will be so much fun to have him here," she said. "I know you'll like him."

That was one prediction that wasn't coming true.

We walked toward the art building as she kept talking about Marco. The morning sun climbed out from behind clouds and dew glistened on the grass. Neither of us had plans for lunch so we agreed to meet by the fountain at noon. I kept close to her and breathed in the citrusy smell of her shampoo.

Marco was coming, and I didn't know what to expect, but I felt energized, more alive. At the fountain, we hugged, and I held her tightly.

I MADE SURE IT WAS AFTER NINE BEFORE GOING home. Mom and Dad would be at work and Lansing would be at the country club carrying golf bags for guys who were too lazy to do it themselves. I checked around to make sure everybody was gone and wished I had someplace else to go.

As I entered, for some reason, I thought about the story about the prodigal son, the one who returns home after being gone for a long time. Nobody was going to welcome me. Nobody was going to shower gifts upon me or throw a party. That story had always seemed so unfair. The son who stays and does what he's supposed to doesn't get anything. But the one who goes away and blows his inheritance gets all the attention when he returns.

In our family, Lansing was the good son. I was the one who went away, though it was only for a couple of days. In some ways, though, I'd been going away for a long time. I wouldn't be the doctor they wanted me to be. I was reminded of the *Sesame Street* game from when I was little, "One of These Things Is Not Like the Others," the one with four boxes where one thing is not the same. That was me. I was so different from the three of them that I felt like I'd been born into the wrong family.

I charged my phone and set the alarm so I'd have time to shower and get ready before lunch. It felt weird to be home by myself as I climbed into bed, but after the hard floor of the classroom, sleep came easy.

I WOKE UP TO MY PHONE RINGING. "Hello."

"Hi, it's Stephanie. Do you have a minute, Cray?"

"Yeah." I sat up in bed and worried that she had had another complaint.

"All your paperwork and references checked out, including rave reviews from Mr. Martinez and Mr. Reinertsen. You're officially hired by CSS."

"Great."

"I've also got morning shifts to fill tomorrow, Thursday, and Friday since Darla called in with a family emergency. Rayne suggested you. Are you interested?"

"Sure." I hadn't worked by myself and she was offering me morning shifts. "Someone would have to explain what I'd need to do, though."

"Rayne can do that when you orientate tonight, and I'll come by in the morning to give meds."

"Okay." Stephanie wasn't holding anything against me after our talk. She was giving me the second chance she'd promised.

"Thanks, Cray. I appreciate your flexibility."

She was the second person that morning to call me flexible.

I'd never thought of myself that way, but maybe I was. I got out of bed and realized I'd done something Dad had asked. He said I needed a job other than "sleeping over." Stephanie had just offered me one. It was only a few small shifts, but it was something to tell him. There were probably more where that came from. I might not have to search for a whole new job.

I went down to the kitchen and poured myself a bowl of Honey Nut Cheerios. As I ate, I thought about what would be okay to take for lunch with Rayne. I searched through the cupboards checking for nonwheat items. All the cookies and crackers contained wheat, including graham crackers, which I'd thought might be okay. Oatmeal-cinnamon granola bars were fine and so was the fruit in the glass bowl on the kitchen island. I picked out two tangerines and a couple of bananas. Rayne would like those. I remembered her eating the walnut on the banana in that sexy way, so I found a bag of nuts in the cupboard. They were pistachios rather than walnuts, but they were wheat-free, so I poured a bunch into a Ziploc bag.

I packed everything and went to shower. I was excited to see Rayne and show her what I had for lunch, our last one together before Marco arrived.

LAYING DOWN THE LAW

"IT'S A FEAST." Rayne checked out the items as we placed them on the concrete wall around the fountain.

"Yeah, we chose things that go together and we didn't even coordinate it."

Rayne smiled. "We coordinated. We just didn't talk about it."

I took a bite of an avocado-and-cheese sandwich. "Where did you get this bread?"

"The co-op has a wheat-free focaccia. Do you like it?"

"Yeah, it's good."

"Try some of these. They're from the garden and have a nice kick." She passed me a container of green beans with hot pepper flakes on them.

I bit into one cautiously but it was tasty. I shelled a pistachio and handed it to her. "How was work this morning?"

"Excellent. I was cataloging images of Charles Rennie Mackintosh. Do you know him?"

"No."

"He was a Scottish architect and designer, and I keep thinking of this one chair he made. The back is like a ladder going to the sky and the seat is rose-colored, a spectacular piece of furniture." Rayne moved her hands around as she discussed the design.

I didn't know anyone who could get so excited about a chair, which was one more thing I liked about her.

"He worked with his wife, the artist Margaret Macdonald. They did some gorgeous watercolors and stained glass together." Rayne shelled another pistachio. "These are good."

"So are these." I held up a green bean.

"Mackintosh designed buildings in Glasgow that I have to see, including the Willow Tea Rooms and the School of Art."

"When are you going?" I'd pushed Rayne's trip to the back of my mind.

"I fly out August thirty-first and arrive September first. Most of the tourists will be gone, and I'll get a better sense of Glasgow."

August 31 was less than three months away! Being in Clairemont without Rayne would be awful.

"I'll spend five days exploring the museums and galleries of Glasgow. Then I'll take the West Highland Line train up through Garelochhead, Crianlarich, and across Rannoch Moor. I'll even cross the Glenfinnan Viaduct, the bridge in the Harry Potter films."

The words rolled off her tongue easily, and I felt like I was listening to a foreign language.

"From Mallaig, I'll catch the ferry and go over the sea to Skye." Rayne's excitement was obvious, and I envied her clarity about her plans. She picked up a tangerine and slowly peeled it in one continuous piece.

"When will you be back?"

"I want to travel as long as I can, at least a year. I'll pick up some side jobs and trade work for room and board. Technically it's illegal to work on a tourist visa, but I know people who've done it and been paid in cash. I'm ready for an adventure."

I unwrapped a granola bar and listened as Rayne talked confidently about what she planned to see.

"There's this bagpiping center in Borreraig that highlights the history of the MacCrimmons, my ancestors. They were the pipers for the MacLeods of Dunvegan Castle, so I've got to go to Dunvegan and Borreraig. Aren't the names brilliant? Don't you want to go there just based on the names?"

"Yeah." And I did. I wanted to go, too.

"Cray, I've got a favor to ask." She looked at me directly. "I know it's last minute, but can you work for me tomorrow night? I asked Stephanie and she said it's fine since it means you'll start one night earlier than you would have. It's Marco's first night here and I have to be with him."

"Okay." I wasn't eager to help them be together, but there was no way to say that without sounding jerkish.

BACK HOME, I checked messages on my phone and waited to see who would show up first. I remembered Dad's *You'll regret it* warning, but so far I hadn't. I sat in the kitchen drumming my fingers on my phone case.

Mom was the first to return, and she gave me a hug. "Oh, Cray, it's so good to see you." She took a long look and her eyes moistened. "We're going out for dinner," she said. "Your pick. Anyplace you want." She acted like I'd been gone for a year and treated me like I was the returning prodigal son.

"Anyplace?"

"Yes, anyplace."

I didn't know how Dad would feel about that.

"Let's go into the living room and sit down." Mom led the way and I followed. "Tell me what you've been doing."

And she actually wanted to know. I told her about Rayne and Stephanie and Oakcrest and my orientation. She listened and nodded and didn't bring up college and how *disappointed* she was. She didn't even warn me about Dad or tell me how angry he'd be.

"I'm glad you're home." She dabbed at her eyes with a tissue, and I believed her.

Lansing came back later from the country club and sat down and asked questions about where I'd been and what I'd been doing. I told him about Oakcrest and he was interested, too.

"We're going out to dinner to celebrate," Mom said.

"Celebrate what?" Lansing asked.

"Celebrate all of us being together," Mom said.

"Where are we going?" Lansing looked to me.

"How about Los Corrales?" I suggested our favorite.

"Awesome." He got up. "I'm going to shower."

Things were going way better than I expected, but I still had Dad to deal with. I wished Mom would have called to tell him I was home, that everything was fine, and that we were going out to dinner. The fewer surprises with him, the better. I checked messages on my phone again while she poured juice spritzers in the kitchen.

"Here's your father," she announced when his car drove up.

I stood up. Then I sat back down. Mom handed me a cranberry spritzer and I took a long drink. I was seventeen years old. I'd graduated from high school and had a job. But I was still afraid of him.

His BMW door slammed and I mouthed a piece of ice and crushed it while Mom made him a gin and tonic.

"Who left the garage door open so leaves blew in?" he asked.

For once it wasn't me.

"I did just now." Mom cut the lime into thin slices the way Dad liked. "It was only ten minutes till you got home."

"Well, close it. There's no reason to leave it open."

I sat there on the couch waiting for him to notice me after he finished listing all the problems that leaves in the garage could cause.

"Cray's here." Mom presented Dad his drink.

"I can see that." Dad took a sip.

"Hi." I shifted on the couch.

"Ehh." He grunted.

"I haven't planned anything for dinner," she said, "so we decided to go to Los Corrales."

"It's too damn noisy there." Dad wiped his mouth.

"We can go someplace else." Mom sat down and encouraged him to as well.

I hated how she always backed down from him. We'd decided where we were going and I wanted her to stick with it.

"Let's go to Manfred's?" He eased into his chair.

"They'll have a line." She knew how much Dad hated to wait. "Los Corrales won't."

My foot tapped an extra-fast beat.

"It's noisy," Dad complained.

"We can sit in back," Mom said. "It's quieter there."

"We've got to be over at Ed's by eight for birthday cake." Dad swirled his drink and gazed into it.

"We'll have plenty of time," she said.

Dad scratched his chin. The bags under his eyes seemed darker. Maybe he hadn't slept well last night, either. "Let's get one thing straight. When you live in this house, you follow certain rules. If you can't, you'll need to find someplace else."

I set my glass down and prepared for his standard lecture.

"Number one," he said, "you'll pay monthly rent like we discussed. Number two, you'll do the things we do as a family, like go to church every Sunday, and I mean every Sunday. Number three, you won't disappear for days on end without letting us know in advance. Do I make myself clear?"

"Yes." There was no negotiating with him. He was laying down the law, and I had to follow it as long as I was in his house. But there were no extra consequences for *You'll regret it.*

Suddenly I realized how Dad's threats had power as long as I did what he wanted. When I didn't, he was unsure what to do.

Dad rubbed his eyes. Maybe the reality that I wasn't going to be a doctor was finally sinking in. For a second, I even felt a little sorry for him.

"You may have graduated," he said, tapping the table in front of him, "but you still follow our rules around here. You don't get to do whatever the hell you want."

The second passed and a familiar feeling returned. The trap was snapping and I desperately needed to get out.

AGE APPROPRIATE

AFTER LISTENING TO DAD, I didn't feel like going out to dinner, but Mom bustled about and talked about how cozy it was to have "just us time" before we went to Uncle Ed's. That sounded terrible, but after Dad's lecture, there was no way I was getting out of it.

At Los Corrales, an older woman rushed up to us. "Dr. Franklin, I'm Carol Gallagher. I'm so happy to see you. You did surgery on my husband, Pat, a year ago, and he's doing great. You saved his life, and I always meant to send you a thank-you."

"That's not necessary," Dad said. "Please give Pat my greetings."

"Yes, I will." She shook Dad's hand vigorously. "Thank you, Dr. Franklin."

I slid into the booth opposite Lansing, and Mom raised her eyebrows in a see-I-told-you way. The waiter brought a basket of chips and a bowl of salsa and I took a handful and set them on my plate. Mom and Dad both ordered margaritas, and Lansing and I got Sprites.

Dad asked me about finding another job and I was glad to tell him I couldn't stay late at Ed's because I had orientation and I'd picked up three morning shifts for the week.

"Are those permanent?"

"No, but more hours are available when people take vacations or call in sick. Stephanie, my supervisor, has other houses where she needs subs."

"You need to get something permanent," Dad said, but it felt more automatic, less like he was ripping into me. Maybe something had shifted. Or possibly he was making an effort since we were out in public.

"Are you getting chilaquiles?" Lansing asked me.

"Definitely." They'd become a favorite since we'd had them in Mexico.

"Me too," he said.

"What other plans besides working do you have for the summer?" Mom asked.

"I want to save some money for a trip." I dipped a chip in salsa.

"Where to?" Lansing asked.

"Europe." I slid back in the booth.

"Europe! You've never mentioned that before," Mom said. "Where in Europe?"

"I was thinking about Scotland."

"You don't want to go to Scotland. It rains all the time," Dad said. "It's a terrible place."

That seemed extreme even for him. "I'd like to see Glasgow and go over to Skye."

"Who would you go with?" Mom asked.

"Maybe my friend Rayne."

"Don't let anybody drag you someplace like Scotland that you've got no reason to go." Dad frowned. "Remember, you need to pay rent. That's what you need to make money for."

"But what about college?" Mom asked. "Why don't you defer a year and live at home and we can straighten things out?"

"There's nothing to straighten out," Dad said. "Cray made his decision. Now he has to pay the price."

I broke the chips on my plate and avoided looking at him.

"You don't have to tell people at Ed's what you're doing," Dad continued. "They don't need to know everything."

What a hypocrite. He wanted me to pay the price for my decision but not tell his brother's family about it. I was sick of playing his games. If I had to pay rent at home, I could take that money and go someplace else, someplace where I was free to make my own rules.

"HAVE SOME CHOCOLATE CAKE." Aunt Laura presented me a piece with lots of frosting. "Do you want ice cream?"

"Please."

My cousin Jeremy, who was a star med student, came over carrying a carton of Häagen-Dazs vanilla. "How many scoops?"

"Two."

"What are you doing this fall?" Jeremy plopped a small mountain of ice cream beside my cake, and Mom watched how I'd answer.

I wasn't lying for Dad. "I'm taking a gap year. Going to do some traveling."

"Good for you," Jeremy said. "I wish I had done that."

I smiled at Mom. That gap year answer was magic. It sounded

like doing something positive rather than avoiding things, and it cut down on the follow-up questions dramatically.

I took a bite of cake and surveyed the room. Uncle Ed was a surgeon. My cousins Jeremy and Jessica were set to be surgeons. Lansing was on his way to being a surgeon. The only other person who wasn't sat down beside me.

"I love cake," Jacob said.

"Yeah, who doesn't?" Then I remembered Rayne. She couldn't eat this. But that didn't mean she didn't love it.

Over by the piano, Dad, Ed, and Jessica argued about insurance reimbursement while Lansing listened.

"Got any new Batman stuff?" I asked Jacob.

"Yeah, I've got two new comic books. You want to see them?"

"Sure."

So after we finished our cake and ice cream, Jacob and I went down to his room and he showed me his Batman stuff. I wondered what Kirsty would say about the age appropriateness of Batman for two seventeen-year-olds. But all kinds of adults were into Batman comics and movies. They dressed up in character and spent thousands of dollars collecting stuff like Jacob had. That was the point of living in America. We were supposed to be free to choose what we wanted.

I picked up a detailed Batman model and turned it over. When we were little, I always got to be Batman and Jacob was Robin. It might be time to switch. "Would you like to be Batman, Jacob?"

"No, you're a good Batman."

So while the rest of the family discussed the future of medicine, Jacob and I teamed up against Catwoman and the Joker, and I felt like I had the best partner in the house.

I RECOGNIZED KIRSTY'S MINIVAN IN THE DRIVEWAY when I arrived at Oakcrest and hoped Rayne was already inside. I was hesitant to talk to Kirsty by myself since this was the first time I'd seen her since she turned me in. I wasn't looking for a confrontation, but I also didn't want to pretend everything was fine. I walked up the steps and paused. I didn't need to ring the doorbell. This was my work. I took a deep breath and opened the door.

On the couch, Rayne sat beside Kirsty holding a ball of purple yarn and a pair of needles. I said hello and they went right back to their knitting tutorial.

Kirsty demonstrated how to hold the needles and Rayne asked questions. I sat down on the other couch and tried to figure out Rayne's new interest. Slowly it dawned on me. Rayne was using knitting as a way to connect. She glanced over and I knew she was letting me know that there was no point in bringing up the complaint.

When Kirsty left she waved good-bye and said, "Have a good orientation." As soon as the door closed, Sean and Nicole came out of their rooms.

"Hi, Race Car," Sean said.

"Kirsty said you're supposed to call me Cray."

"Kirsty's not here. Rayne is." Nicole sat down.

"She won't care, will you, Rayne?" Sean sat down in the chair next to her.

"No," Rayne said. "Just call him Cray when Kirsty's around."

"Okay." Sean looked over at me. "How you been, Race Car?"

"Good." My new name had stuck.

"I just got another Justin Bieber poster, Race Car," Nicole said. "You want to see it?"

"Sure." I walked down to her room and she showed me how she'd taped it inside her closet, the only place she still had room. "Nice. You can't have too much Bieb."

On the way back, Kate peeked out of her doorway.

"Race Car's here," Nicole said.

As I sat down on the couch with Rayne, Kate came out in her robe and slippers holding Chimney.

"We've got everybody here but Brent," Nicole said.

"He's sleeping." Sean tapped his feet.

"He always goes to bed early," Nicole said.

"Knock, knock," Sean said.

"Come in." Kate giggled as she sat down next to Nicole. I was starting to understand her better.

"No, you say *who's there*," Sean said. "Knock, knock."

"Who's there?" we all said together.

"Harry."

"Harry who?"

"Harry up and open the door. It's freezing out." Sean laughed deeply like this was the funniest joke in the world, and we all laughed at his laugh.

"I've got one," I said. "Say the word *most* five times fast."

"Most, most, most, most, most," everybody repeated.

"Now what do you put in a toaster?"

"Toast," Sean and Nicole shouted.

"Toast," Kate said.

I turned to Rayne.

"Toast," she agreed.

"Nah." I shook my head. "You put bread in a toaster."

"Ahhh," everybody groaned.

We took turns telling jokes and laughed the hardest at one Nicole told about a monkey on a trampoline where she mixed up the punch line.

After Sean, Kate, and Nicole said good night, Rayne showed me where things were and went through the morning orientation. She pointed to the schedule that Darla, the morning person, had made that listed the times people got up, when their transportation arrived, and the phone numbers to call with any problems.

"Everybody is good about getting ready and will make their own breakfast," Rayne said. "Brent's often unsteady at first and you may have to remind Nicole to take her lunch and Brent to brush his teeth. If anybody's shampoo goes missing, have Sean search through his collection and return it." She paused at the closet door. "And since you're not med certified, Stephanie will come in to give meds."

I worried about remembering everything, but if I forgot something I could always ask the people who lived here. They knew how things worked.

"I had a good talk with Kirsty." Rayne sat down on the couch in the living room. "She was pleased with how you helped with Brent."

"Then why did she turn me in?" I sat down across from her.

"That's the way she is," Rayne said. "She's close to Rebecca and misses her. She was going to have problems with anyone who filled in. She said you were okay, so you've passed her test."

I wanted to protest about the stupidity of her age-appropriateness complaint, but it didn't seem necessary.

"At night when you come in, Sean, Kate, and Nicole might come down like they did tonight. If they stay in their rooms, that means they want their privacy. Only go in if you're invited. If they come down, they'll talk for a while and then go to bed. After that, the time is yours."

Rayne switched to the topic of Marco and how excited she was to see him. I didn't need to hear more about her older Italian photographer boyfriend, so I wasn't paying attention, but then she mentioned me.

"The three of us can meet for dinner on Thursday. That will be fun."

I didn't think so. Not one bit.

MEETING MARCO

WEDNESDAY NIGHT, I pulled down the sheets on the same bed that Rayne slept in four nights a week at Oakcrest. My gray gym shorts and Clairemont Hoops T-shirt looked worn and I wondered what she wore. Maybe something sexy, some thin nightgown. Maybe nothing at all.

I was working for her so she could be with Marco, and I imagined what the two of them were doing. I held the pillow and inhaled. Even though the bed had been stripped and I'd put clean sheets and pillowcases on, I still felt like I could smell her. I wanted to believe that, anyway.

To take my mind off them, I grabbed Rayne's guidebook to Skye. On a bookmarked page was a picture of a bagpiper in a kilt identified as Patrick MacCrimmon, one of the hereditary pipers to the MacLeods of Dunvegan. I looked closely to see if I could see a resemblance between that MacCrimmon and Rayne. They both were thin and dark, but I wouldn't have guessed he was an ancestor if she hadn't told me.

I paged through the book and came to a picture of the ruins of

Trumpan Church. I read the description of what happened there in 1577. A raiding party of MacLeods trapped a group of MacDonalds in a cave on the island of Eigg. The MacLeods started a fire in the entrance and suffocated 395 MacDonalds, the entire island population.

In retaliation, other MacDonalds attacked Trumpan Church, where the MacLeods had gathered for Sunday services. The MacDonalds blocked the doors and lit the thatched roof on fire. All the MacLeods inside but one died. A young girl squeezed through a window and escaped. She ran toward Dunvegan and sounded the alarm. MacLeod warriors mobilized and murdered every single MacDonald.

I studied the picture of the church ruins among green grass by open water. What a contrast with its violent past. The more I read about the battles and retaliations, the more I realized that underneath this peaceful landscape, the soil was soaked in blood.

I flipped to another page and read about the Talisker Distillery near Carbost on the west side of the island. Guests were welcome to sample whisky prior to taking the distillery tour and the drinking age was only eighteen. Bagpipes, battles, whisky—Skye was a place I wanted to go. Maybe that's why Rayne had left the book out, so I'd get interested. I hoped she was still going there and not to Italy with Marco.

IN THE MORNING, Brent ate a brown sugar cinnamon Pop-Tart out of the package. He hadn't done a good job shaving but I was afraid to tell him.

"Where's Darla?" he asked with his mouth full.

"She had a family emergency. I'll be here the next couple of mornings."

Kate took out a box of frozen waffles and put one in the toaster. They looked good and nobody seemed to need my help, so I put in a couple for myself.

Sean said that he ate at McDonald's and they had the best breakfasts. He then proceeded to list every item on the breakfast menu.

"Big deal. You tell us that all the time." Brent left his wrapper on the counter.

"I never told Race Car," Sean insisted.

I pointed at the wrapper and Brent put it in the trash.

"Good morning." Stephanie came in carrying a large coffee.

Everybody said hello, and she turned to me.

"How'd your night go, Cray?"

"Good." I poured maple syrup over my waffles. I was getting paid to sleep *and* eat.

"Thanks for covering for Rayne. I know how important it was for her to have the night off." She unlocked the closet door and used another key to open the med cabinet. She counted out Brent's pills into a small paper cup.

Brent gulped them down with water. "I miss Rebecca being here."

"I'm sure she misses you, too. She'll be back in September." Stephanie took a sip from her cup. "Remember to do a good job on your teeth and check your chin. You missed some spots shaving."

"I will. I will." He headed for the bathroom.

Stephanie gave Nicole vitamins and calmed Kate down when she was biting her arm by telling her she'd join her at Walmart for her performance review. She also reminded Sean about his doctor's appointment after work. I was impressed by how much she kept track of and how she delivered information in such an easy way.

"Nicole, your van is here," Sean called out like a conductor.

"Bye." Nicole grabbed her stuff and hurried out.

Sean continued watching at the front window. "Sean's van is now here," he announced. "Hey, Race Car, why was the broom late?"

"I don't know."

"Because it overswept. Get it?" He bounded down the stairs.

"Yeah. Have a good day."

After everybody left, Stephanie and I sat down in the living room.

"You're doing well, Cray. You've recovered from your initial mistake the way I hoped, and you work well with the people we support."

"Thanks." I hadn't gotten that feedback before.

"I'm already thinking ahead to the fall." Stephanie finished her coffee.

"What do you mean?"

"Rebecca's coming back, but Rayne's leaving us at the end of August and I need someone to fill her full-time spot. Are you interested in being considered for a permanent position?"

I looked up. "I don't know." I'd just started and Stephanie was offering me more. I should have been grateful, but the word *permanent* scared me, as if I'd be doing it forever.

"Think about it," Stephanie said. "You'd be eligible for health insurance, dental coverage, and vacation."

"Okay." I stretched out my feet in front of me. If Rayne was traveling, though, I wanted to do that, too. But not with Marco.

THAT EVENING I ARRIVED DOWNTOWN AT A TINY restaurant called Adrianna's that I'd never been to. I paused at the aqua door and felt like running away.

Inside, my eyes adjusted to the dark and I saw the two of them sitting across from each other laughing.

"You must be Cray." A tall guy with long black hair stood up.

"Hi." I held up my hand like a little kid learning to wave and felt like a dork.

"Hey, Cray." Rayne gave me a hug.

I looked back and forth between them and wasn't sure where to sit. I wanted to be next to Rayne, but that might not be what she wanted. I stood there, hesitating, afraid of making a wrong move.

"Please." Marco pulled out the chair next to him. He was wearing jeans and a T-shirt but looked more stylish than anybody in Clairemont.

I glanced across at Rayne, who smiled broadly, like she couldn't be happier to have him back.

"I'm so glad to meet you," Marco said in slightly accented English as he held out his hand.

"Thanks." I shook it firmly. I wanted to dislike him, but he wasn't giving me much to work with.

"We love this place," Rayne said. "Adrianna makes the best arepas."

"What are they?" I asked.

"Round corn cakes that are split in half and filled with different ingredients. They're the main food in Venezuela, where she's from."

"My favorite is the slow-roasted pork," Marco said.

Rayne obviously hadn't made a vegetarian of him. I studied the menu and decided to go with the black beans and cheese ones.

The waitress brought Marco a beer. When I ordered a Sprite, that made the age gap between us even more obvious.

Marco and Rayne knew the waitress, and he ordered in Spanish from her. I did, too, when my turn came and was pleased when Rayne chose what I had.

"Your Spanish is very good," Marco said to me.

"Thanks, so is yours."

"Spanish and Italian are close, so it's not difficult."

"I wish I'd taken Spanish," Rayne said.

When Marco got up to wash his hands, I looked across at Rayne.

"How's it going?" I asked.

"It's fantastic to have him here."

That was exactly what I'd feared. I knew we didn't have much time before he returned, and I blurted out what was on my mind. "Where's he sleeping?"

"In my bed." Rayne looked at me like that was the dumbest question she'd ever heard.

"Your dad's cool with that?"

"Of course. We're lovers. He knows we have sex."

Immediately I regretted asking and felt like a kid again.

When Marco returned, he and Rayne talked about photography and film, and I mainly listened since I didn't have much to add. They both were excited about something they'd seen called *The Clock*, which was twenty-four hours long.

"It's about time and the history of cinema," Rayne said, "but it's about so much else."

"Exactly." Marco moved his hands for emphasis. "It's sex and love and life and death."

As they talked, I realized how perfect they were for each other. Rayne had found a guy who loved the same things she did.

When the food came, Marco turned to me and asked if we could speak in Spanish.

"*Si.*"

He looked at Rayne and said, *She likes to be right, doesn't she?* I nodded and he said, *She likes to be in control, too.*

"Are you two talking about me?" Rayne said. "If so, you need to switch back to English immediately."

"See what I mean," Marco said in English. "We were saying you have strong opinions."

"Is that a problem?" She took a drink of water.

"No, not usually. But sometimes it's important to trust people and go along with them." Marco wiped pork from his lips with his napkin. "What do you think, Cray?"

I didn't know what he was getting at, but I knew how I felt about Rayne. "I like it that Rayne knows what she wants. It's cool she's willing to be different and try things other people wouldn't. We need more different around here." I glanced over at her and caught a slight smile.

"Yes," Marco said. "But there are times when it's important to trust others, especially when it's people we love."

He and Rayne went back and forth for a while and were obviously talking about something between them. I felt like I was on the outside looking in, so I concentrated on my arepas, which were surprisingly good.

After we ate, Marco asked if I'd ever been to Italy.

"No, I've never even been to Europe."

"You've got to come. You'll love it. And when you do you can stay with us in Modena. You're welcome anytime."

Later I realized I wasn't sure who the *us* referred to. Was it Marco and his parents? Or was it him and Rayne?

Had they already decided their future together?

ZERO

WHEN I GOT TO OAKCREST LATER THAT NIGHT, Sean and Nicole were finishing up a game of Uno with Eli, who was subbing for Kirsty.

"I won." Sean raised his arms triumphantly.

"You cheated," Nicole said.

"I did not. You have to say 'Uno' when you only have one card or you have to draw two new ones, don't you, Eli?"

"That's right." Eli gathered up the cards as Sean and Nicole argued, and I sat down on the couch.

"We can play again tomorrow," Sean said.

"We'll see about that. I'm going to bed," Nicole announced.

Sean discussed his win and then went down to his room, too.

Eli turned to me. "How are you liking Oakcrest?"

"Good. I've got lots to learn, but I like being here."

"It takes time. You're off to a good start."

"Thanks."

"I heard from Rayne you're not going to college this fall."

"Yeah."

"That takes guts. Too many people go because they feel they're supposed to without thinking about what they really want. Half the time, they're doing it for their parents, not for themselves." He rubbed his chin.

"What about you? Are you planning to go back sometime?"

"Yeah, I'll definitely get my degree, but right now I'm learning a lot here and being in the band and improving as a musician and songwriter. It's all good." Eli put his guitar in its case and clicked it shut and gathered up his stuff.

"See you tomorrow, Race Car," he said as he went out.

"See you, Eli."

After he left, my thoughts turned back to Rayne and Marco. That conversation with Marco in Spanish had been weird, and something was going on, but no matter how much I replayed it, I couldn't figure it out.

FRIDAY NIGHT, as I was sitting in my room watching Vines on my laptop, my phone rang. It was Rayne.

"What's up?" I tried to sound casual.

But she didn't say anything. Instead I heard the deepest, most painful crying, like a wounded animal.

"Rayne, what's going on? Are you okay?"

"Nnnnn." The crying continued.

"Do you need help?"

She kept crying.

"Rayne, tell me what happened."

Eventually I was able to make out some words between the sobbing.

"Gone . . . ended . . . asshole."

"I'm sorry," I said.

"Can you come, Cray? I need you."

"Yeah, definitely."

"I'm at the cemetery."

"I'm on my way." I ran as fast as I could and worried about what Marco had done to her.

I SAW HER STANDING BY THE GATE. She wiped her red, puffy eyes on her sleeve.

"What happened?"

"We had a terrible fight."

"Did he hit you?"

"No, nothing like that, but it was awful."

"What happened?" I handed her a tissue from the pack I'd grabbed.

"Marco wants me in Modena and can't understand why I'm not there. He's taking it personally that I'm going to Scotland by myself instead of coming to Italy to meet his parents. He's talking marriage and how much fun it would be to have a bambino." She blew her nose. "I'm not close to being ready to have a kid. I still feel like a kid myself."

We walked along the paved path past gravestones, and the talking seemed to calm her down.

"Something changed when Marco went back. He's getting pressure from his mom, who's in a hurry to become a grandma, and rather than stand up to her, he's going along with it. He's acting much more traditional, and he came all this way to persuade me to come back with him, but that's not what I want."

Rayne wiped her eyes again with her sleeve so I handed her another tissue.

"He didn't listen to anything I said about how important it is for me to go to Scotland. He said Italy is sunnier and warmer and the food is much better, which isn't the point at all."

We continued past Mr. Driggs's and Zoran's graves but didn't stop.

"He was being selfish, but when I said that he called me a selfish bitch and started swearing in Italian. I kind of lost it and called him an arrogant asshole and other names and he made a bunch of accusations."

"Where's he now?" I asked.

"Gone. He took a van to the airport to fly back. He's gone."

"Really?" I stared in disbelief. He was supposed to stay a week, but he hadn't made it half that time.

"He accused me of liking you more than I liked him."

"What?" That sounded crazy.

"I told him that based on the way he was acting, I did, and that made him even madder. I said you weren't trying to control my life."

"You told him you liked me better?"

"Yeah."

"But you were having sex with him."

"I was, but that's over. Done. *Finito*." She clapped her hands together.

We reached the end of the cemetery and started looping back. I couldn't believe it. Rayne wasn't going to Italy. She was done with Marco. She liked me better.

"You saved me, Cray. I didn't know what I was going to do with Marco gone."

"You saved me." I stopped. "I couldn't imagine this summer without you."

"Me too." She reached out and gave me a hug. It felt so good

to hold her body against mine. I held her tightly but then remembered something. I pulled back and checked my phone.

"Oh shit. It's five to ten. I'm supposed to be at Oakcrest." I started
running down the path.

"I'll call Kirsty," Rayne hollered. "I'll tell her you were helping me."

I SIPPED A LARGE ICED COFFEE AT THE EDGE WHILE I
kept a saucer on top of Rayne's tea to keep it hot.

When she walked in, I gave her a hug.

"Thanks again for last night," she said. "I'm less a mess today."

"You look good."

"Thanks for the tea, too." She blew on it and took a sip. "How'd
your night go?"

"Fine. Kirsty said she was okay with me being late." I leaned
back. I felt bolder with Marco gone and after Rayne had said she
liked me better. I shook the ice in my coffee. "I've decided something big."

"What?"

"Stephanie said she'd consider me for your full-time position
this fall, but I'm not interested."

"Why not?" Rayne looked puzzled.

"I've been thinking. It doesn't make sense for me to pay rent to
Dad when I could take that money and travel. The way they're acting, they should be paying me to stay with them."

Rayne laughed. "Where do you want to go?"

"Skye," I said confidently.

"Skye?"

"I've been reading your guidebook. I want to see Scotland, too.
We could go together."

Rayne shook her head.

"What's the matter?"

"That's not possible."

"Why not?" I'd expected her to be excited.

"I need to do this on my own," she said.

"Why?" I felt like the floor had gone out beneath me.

"This is my trip, a solo trip. First Marco, now you. I don't know why it's so hard for you guys to understand."

"I'm not him," I said loudly. "You were clear about that last night."

"I know, but it's not about you. This is about me. I need to make this trip for myself. I don't want a traveling companion."

I stood up and threw my cup in the trash.

"I'm sorry," Rayne called.

I didn't respond as I slammed the door behind me. *Traveling companion. Traveling companion.* That sounded so pathetic. I wasn't interested in being her *traveling companion.* After last night, I wanted way more from her than that.

For the next three days, I blocked out Rayne. No phone calls. No texts. No IMs. Nothing. I didn't see her at Oakcrest either since we worked on different nights. Not talking to her ripped me up, but talking to her would have been worse. I needed her to know how angry I was.

I slept a lot and stayed in my room playing video games. Mom noticed and asked about it, but I said I was fine. I was killing time, which was a strange expression. It wasn't time's fault I felt so shitty.

I kept circling back to Rayne's comparison of me and Marco and her *traveling companion* crack. It sounded like I was some hopeless, lonely person. If that was how she felt, I'd been delusional about what was happening between us and she'd just used me that night in the cemetery when her wounds from Marco were fresh. Maybe I'd totally misunderstood how she saw me.

I struggled to figure out what I would do. I might have to consider Stephanie's offer of the full-time job. I might have to pay rent at home until I saved enough to move out. That permanent job at Oakcrest might be what I'd do for my gap life.

A couple of times I picked up my phone and came close to calling Jett, but I couldn't handle telling him what had happened. He and Nora had warned me about Rayne, and I hated to admit they'd been right.

When my first paycheck was finally deposited into my account, I went down to the bank and withdrew the money. The teller gave me an envelope of cash and I didn't even count it. Instead I took it home to Dad, who was looking at his iPad in the kitchen. I handed it to him and said, "Here's my rent."

"Okay." He set it on the table and kept reading.

It was as if he was getting paid for my work at Oakcrest, which completely sucked. If that was supposed to force me to go to college on his terms, it was backfiring.

I continued to work my nights at Oakcrest. I enjoyed hanging out with the people there and they seemed to like having me around. Brent talked less about missing Rebecca. Sean volunteered to show me his shampoo collection of 106 bottles lined up around his room, all with shampoo in them so he'd never run out. I was even getting more comfortable with Kate and her silence. She seemed to pick up on that and wasn't quite so anxious.

On Father's Day, I went through the motions of giving Dad a card, new golf balls and tees, and a blue-checked tie that Mom picked out. He said thanks, but we all knew what he really wanted:

me enrolling at St. Luke's and studying premed. That wasn't happening, so the other gifts felt pretty small.

I kept reviewing how I'd misread Rayne's intentions about Scotland. I'd made a fool of myself and hated how she'd compared me to Marco. He hadn't realized why Scotland was so important to her, and I had. But we both wanted her to do what we wanted without hearing what she needed.

I'd hoped traveling with her would solve things. Now I was back to zero.

ON THE BRIDGE

TUESDAY EVENING, as I was wheeling the trash bin to the curb, my phone buzzed and it was her. I gave in and answered.

"Eli's band is playing an all-ages show tonight at the Main Stage at eight," Rayne said. "Everybody from Oakcrest is going, and Stephanie said you should join us."

I paused. I wanted her to apologize, not act like nothing was going on between us.

"Cray?"

"Yeah." I breathed in rotting garbage.

"Can you meet us?"

I didn't respond. I had no desire to go, but if Stephanie wanted me to, I probably should. I owed her for giving me a second chance. "Okay. I'll be there." I was ready to disconnect. But I hung on for one more beat.

"I can't wait." Rayne ended the call.

I debated whether Rayne was playing games, whether she was manipulating me the way she said Nora was with Jett. Part of me wanted to stay mad at her and part of me wanted to get past it. Those two parts were at war and I didn't know which would win.

AT THE CLUB, THE SMELL OF STALE BEER HIT ME AS I looked around. Onstage, equipment was set up, but nobody was playing, and a small crowd gathered waiting for something to happen. I wished I was back outside.

"Cray."

I turned to see Stephanie, Rayne, Kirsty, and an older woman who had to be Darla, the morning person, standing in back. As I walked past beat-up tables, I wished the others were somewhere else so I could talk to Rayne alone. She was wearing jeans and her cracked peace sign T-shirt, which seemed appropriate considering our fight.

"Glad you could make it." Stephanie stepped forward. "Come meet Darla."

"Hi." I shook Darla's wrinkled hand.

"Pleasure to meet you, Cray." She had a soft, grandmotherly quality about her.

"Nicole, Sean, Brent, and Kate are backstage with Eli," Rayne said. "He's introducing them to the band."

"I hope that's all he's introducing them to," Kirsty added.

"They should be back soon." Rayne acted like there wasn't anything special between us. I wondered if that was because work people were around or if there really wasn't. Maybe I'd been so desperate I'd made it all up.

With a burst of noise, Brent, Nicole, Sean, and Kate rushed across the floor. They were all talking at once.

"Eli's dedicating a song to us," Brent said.

"The drummer. I forgot his name. He said I have good jokes."

Sean shifted from one foot to the other like he couldn't wait to dance.

"His name is Zeke," Nicole said.

"Zebra?" Kate questioned.

"Zeke," Nicole repeated.

Brent looked over at me. "Hey, Race Ca—" He stopped when Rayne elbowed him. "I mean Cray."

"I wish Justin Bieber was here. Then the place would be packed." Nicole looked around.

"I think he had other plans tonight," Stephanie said.

The band came out and launched into their first song and were tight. Eli bounced around the stage and the other band members followed his lead. For someone who was so low-key at work, he was full of energy onstage. Sean and Nicole rushed out to dance and Eli encouraged others to join them.

"Let's dance." Stephanie waved everybody forward.

"Not me." Kate shook her head.

"I don't dance." Brent backed up.

"I'll stay with them," Darla said.

"Me too," Kirsty added. "You three go out."

So Stephanie, Rayne, and I moved onto the dance floor with Sean and Nicole. I noticed people watching and wished I'd stayed back with Brent and Kate. Stephanie swirled around and Rayne danced energetically. I moved back and forth awkwardly, but then Nicole came over and danced in front of me. She grinned, but I felt miserable, even as I pretended to be having fun.

Eli took the mic and announced that he was dedicating the next song, "A Bitter Love," to his friends at Oakcrest. Sean and Nicole whooped and hollered and other people clapped. I watched Eli—he seemed bigger and more alive onstage and was totally into it. He'd taken time off from school and found exactly what he wanted to do.

Partway through, I realized Eli was singing about "A Bit of Love," not "A Bitter Love." Rayne slid over to dance in front of me, and Nicole shifted to Stephanie. Rayne and I edged back and forth, getting closer, but not touching. The doubt in my mind lessened as my body pulled me to her. We locked eyes, and both of us seemed to be saying the same thing—enough of the silent treatment. We needed a bit of love ourselves.

AFTER WE'D CONGRATULATED ELI AND THE BAND ON the show, Rayne and I walked down to the pedestrian bridge over the river.

"Every year it amazes me how far north the sun is at the solstice." She stopped and pointed. "See how it's directly above the river?"

I couldn't believe she was talking about the sun. "What the hell's going on with you?"

"Sorry." She rubbed her forehead. "I shouldn't have compared you with Marco. That was unfair."

"Yeah, and what about the 'traveling companion' thing?" We crossed the bridge and turned to walk along the path on the other side.

"I'm sorry about that, too. That came out wrong." Rayne slowed to let me catch up. "What about you? Ghosting me for three days?"

"I was mad. I didn't know what else to do."

"Yeah, I was, too, and said some mean things, so I apologized. How about you?"

"Yeah, I'm sorry for not talking to you."

"Okay. That's done."

Even though things still gnawed at me, I wanted to let them go. When we got to the railroad bridge, we decided to cross. Trains hardly used it and Rayne wanted to be in the middle to watch the setting sun.

"Marco's been Skyping me every day," she said. "He's having a hard time accepting that it's over. He's used to persuading people, especially women, to do what he wants, and he can't quite believe that I'm not going to."

I watched ducks flapping about in the water. I still was amazed that it was really over between them.

"But enough about him," Rayne said. "How about you? What's happening with your dad?"

I told her that he'd backed off since I'd started paying rent and we'd been avoiding talking about college. "I think he and Mom still expect me to cave and accept their terms for next year."

"Look." Rayne stopped on the tracks and we watched the sun drop into the river. "There's only a few days each summer when it does this and I wanted you to see."

The sun looked so much like a burning ball that I half expected it to steam. I had a sudden wish for a train to cross the bridge so Rayne and I would have to grab each other and press against the side, but when I peered down the track, nothing was coming.

I turned to look at her, and as I did, she grabbed me and pulled me toward her. Our lips met and she kissed me hard and I responded. Our tongues touched and I tasted her minty mouth. Her body pressed against mine and I pulled her closer as I ran my hand through her short hair. She slid her hand down and rubbed me through my jeans. I just about lost it but kept my mouth glued to hers as I turned to give her more room. She squeezed me and I gasped. I moved my hand underneath her T-shirt and fumbled with the hook of her bra trying to get it open.

Suddenly, she stepped back and straightened her shirt. "I shouldn't have done that."

"What?" I was dying for more.

"Sorry. It's too soon. I'm still reacting to Marco. I need to break up with him properly. I need to separate from him and have some time." She turned and started down the tracks.

"Don't go!" I couldn't believe that something I'd anticipated for so long could end so quickly.

"I made a mistake."

"It wasn't a mistake, Rayne!" I touched my lips, which had just been on hers. Had I kissed her wrong? Was she turned off by me? Did I move too suddenly when I went for her bra and couldn't get it unhooked?

No! No! No! This wasn't the right ending.

BREAKING UP PROPERLY

THAT KISS AND OUR DESPERATE GRABBING TOLD ME that Rayne and I wanted the same thing. But when I showed up at the fountain the next day with lunch from Subway, she insisted she needed to slow down and "end things properly" with Marco.

"He's been so important to me," she said. "I owe it to him and to myself to do this right."

I held out her salad with extra olives and jalapeno peppers. I'd never known anybody to be so concerned about breaking up properly.

"Marco helped me become more independent." Rayne opened the lid.

"What do you mean? You're incredibly independent." I took a bite of my tuna sandwich.

Rayne shook her head. "Without my mom, I'd been extra dependent on my dad. With Marco, I became more independent from him."

I caught a piece of falling tomato and popped it in my mouth. I'd never thought of her needing to be independent from her dad. She had so much figured out.

"Relationships can be so hard," Rayne said. "At best, they're a sticky mess."

I turned to her. "Do you mean what I think you do?"

She nodded and we both laughed.

"I need a good ending with Marco." Rayne took a drink from her water bottle. "A good ending is the first step in a good beginning."

I wanted to reach out and grab her but I knew she wasn't ready. So I ate my sandwich as she went on about Marco. I tried to listen, not because I was some kind of great guy, but because I so badly wanted that ending to be our beginning.

ONE NIGHT AT THE END OF JUNE, I was reading staff notes on the laptop when Nicole came into the room clutching her finger and gritting her teeth.

"What's the matter?" I asked.

"I cut my finger."

"How?" Blood was the last thing I wanted to deal with.

"Opening my new poster."

"Opening it with what?"

"A kitchen knife."

"Why did you use that?" The word *knife* and the thought of blood were enough to make me feel faint.

"The plastic was tight," Nicole said irritably.

I knew I shouldn't be getting angry and instead should be checking her finger, but I worried if I looked closely I'd fall to the floor. I was feeling woozy already, but I was supposed to be in charge, and nobody in the house knew I had a problem with blood.

"Let's go down to the bathroom and clean it out."

"It hurts," she complained.

"It's going to be okay. Wash it good with soap and water." I sorted through the medicine cabinet, checking for sterilized pads, disinfectant, and Band-Aids. I glanced over at the sink and saw a thin trail of bloody water snaking down. I turned back to the medicine cabinet and started counting Band-Aids. I couldn't let Nicole see how bad I was around blood. *Five, six, seven.*

I tore open a sterilized pad and wrapped it around her finger to dry it without looking. I needed to check to see if she needed stitches, but I wasn't sure I could do that. I applied the disinfectant, and from the feel of the cut, it didn't seem too bad. I took a quick look and saw that it wasn't deep. I opened up a Band-Aid and wound it around her finger.

"Thanks," Nicole said.

"You're welcome." I picked up the wrappers and threw them in the trash.

"You're a good nurse, Race Car." Nicole touched her finger gently.

"Sorry I got mad." I put the unused stuff back in the medicine cabinet.

"That's okay."

"Where are you putting another poster anyway?"

"On the ceiling. Eli's going to help me so when I'm in bed, I'll look up and see Justin."

"You're the biggest Belieber."

"I am." She turned to go back to her room. "Thanks, Race Car."

"You're welcome. Sleep well."

I sat down on the couch and thought about the amazing job I'd fallen into. While I was worried about Nicole seeing my reaction to blood, she was reassuring me that I'd done a good job.

Oakcrest was incredible. The people I was supposed to help were helping me. And they didn't care one bit whether I was going to college or becoming a doctor.

THAT WEEK I WORKED MY NIGHTS AND PICKED UP A couple of extra evening shifts for people on vacation. Rayne and I got together once for lunch, once for dinner, and once to walk around downtown before she had to be at Oakcrest. She kept talking about making progress with Marco, and nothing she said indicated any change in her decision to break up. I definitely wanted it to go faster, but I liked the destination.

On July Fourth, Sean, Nicole, and I went downtown to the courthouse square for an afternoon concert. Brent and Kate were with their families for the long weekend and I was working for Kirsty. We were excited because Rayne had the day off from her art department job and was meeting us.

As we approached the square, I saw Jett and Nora leaving Sam's Pizza. Jett looked over and I raised my arm hesitantly. I hadn't spoken to him since we'd had the argument about Rayne.

He grabbed Nora and came over. I introduced Sean and Nicole as people I worked with.

"Are you here by yourself?" Nora asked.

"No, I'm here with Sean and Nicole." I knew she meant Rayne but I was irritated by how she acted like they were invisible.

"Why do birds fly south?" Sean turned to Jett.

"I don't know."

"Because it's too far to walk." Sean broke into his deep laugh and Jett smiled. Nora pretended to be interested in Sean and Nicole after what I'd said, but I could tell she was faking.

"We've got to go. We're meeting Rayne." I smiled at Nora.

We searched around and picked a shady spot. Sean scurried out to dance even though the music was a brass band playing old-timey songs. Nicole counted her change slowly to make sure she had enough and went off to get ice cream.

A few minutes later Rayne showed up in a tight red, white, and blue T-shirt. "Happy Independence Day."

"Nice shirt." I continued studying it.

"Thanks."

Nicole came back with her ice-cream sandwich and gave Rayne a hug. The band stopped playing and an old veteran spoke about the importance of protecting our independence. I remembered what Rayne had said about Marco helping her become more independent from her dad. That's what she was doing for me, helping me become more independent from *my* dad.

Sitting there listening to the veteran talk about bravery, courage, and freedom, I knew I had to do more. To be free, I needed to be braver and more courageous. I had to push myself to be more independent. I couldn't follow Rayne to Scotland. I had to take a risk myself.

I was saving a little money from my job and had some more in the bank. I still had my passport from our spring break trip to Mexico.

With Rayne leaving, I needed to go someplace in September, too. I closed my eyes and decided where.

THE DISAPPEARANCE

AFTER THE SPEECHES, the band resumed playing and Nicole went out to dance with Sean. I slid closer to Rayne. "When's your flight to Scotland again?"

"The last day of August. I fly Delta overnight to Amsterdam and then KLM to Glasgow. I'm getting so excited."

I picked up a leaf. "I'm going to travel this fall, too."

Rayne held up her hand like she was stopping traffic. "Cray, we talked about this and I made it clear. I need to go on my own."

"Go. Nobody's stopping you. I'm going on my own, too."

"Where?" she asked.

"Spain." I tried to say it like I'd decided longer ago than ten minutes.

"Spain? Why Spain?"

"It's the obvious choice. I've taken Spanish for seven years, and Señor Martinez says the best way to improve is to be in a country where you speak it all the time. We talked about Spain a lot in class, and there are all kinds of places that I want to see. Besides, I need to get out of here if you won't be around. I need to do this for myself, too."

"Are you really going?" Rayne looked doubtful.

"Yeah." I tried to sound confident.

"You don't know anybody there, do you?"

"No, but I'll meet people. I'll figure it out."

She stared at me with her brown eyes and I hoped she was seeing me in a new way. I forgot about everything else and wanted to grab her and kiss her all over.

Rayne broke her gaze and leaned forward. "Where's Nicole?"

"Out dancing."

"I don't see her." Rayne stood up and I did, too. I couldn't see Nicole anywhere as we rushed over to Sean.

"Where's Nicole?" we said together.

"She was dancing with some guy." Sean wiped his forehead.

"Where is he?" I asked.

Sean looked around. "He's gone."

"Stay right here." Rayne pointed to a spot. "Cray and I will find her."

A stab of panic shot through me. I was in charge and I'd lost Nicole.

Rayne pulled out her phone, found Nicole's number, and called, but I could hear from the ringing that there was no answer.

"Nicole, it's Rayne. Call me right away!" she shouted at the voice mail.

"What should we do?" I asked.

"We've got to find her."

I scanned the crowd. No Nicole. "Should we call Stephanie?"

"No. You go that way and we'll meet back here in five minutes."

I hurried through the crowd, getting more and more desperate. If we didn't find her quickly, we'd be in serious trouble. I should have been paying attention instead of trying to impress Rayne.

When we met back, Rayne was questioning Sean.

"We should tell the police." Sean pointed to a cop.

"Not yet," Rayne said.

"Sean, what did the guy she was dancing with look like?" I asked.

"He was short and bald and wore a red headband and maybe a red shirt or maybe it was brown or orange."

I checked everybody who was wearing red, brown, or orange and the person next to them.

"You've got to call Stephanie," Rayne announced.

I got out my phone. "What should I say?"

"Tell her where you are and that you lost Nicole."

I called Stephanie's number but hoped she wouldn't answer. That wouldn't solve anything, but I dreaded telling her.

"Hello," she said.

"It's me, Cray, and I'm in the park across from the courthouse with Sean and Rayne and . . . we can't . . . locate Nicole."

"What? You've *lost* Nicole?"

"Yeah."

"Tell the police. Give them a description. I'll call some staff to come search. She's a vulnerable adult and we've got to find her."

I hung up and felt terrible. The words *vulnerable adult* made Nicole sound helpless in the face of all kinds of danger.

"There's the police," Sean said.

So I gave a description of Nicole to a cop who wrote down my name and phone number. Rayne let me do all the talking, which pissed me off. She could have added something.

When Stephanie showed up, she said she'd notified Gail, which made me feel even worse. Stephanie directed me to check any stores downtown that were open. She sent Rayne and Sean over to the university and Eli, who'd rushed over from band practice, to the river. As soon as I heard that, I hoped he wouldn't find her in the water.

I went from one store to another, but all of them were closed for the holiday. I ran all the way down to the Edge, which was open, but Nicole wasn't inside. My search felt pointless. With every locked door, I got more scared. Something terrible could be happening to Nicole, and it was my fault.

I was in charge and I'd failed to protect her. I remembered Stephanie's words: *One more mistake and you'll be fired.* I'd get fired for sure, and I deserved to, no matter how much I liked the job.

After half an hour of feeling desperate, the only other place I could think to check was Subway. I ran all the way across the bridge. At a booth in back, a short, bald guy wearing a red-and-brown shirt and red headband slurped a drink. Scenarios raced through my mind. He'd raped Nicole and killed her and then disposed of the body. But he didn't have any blood on his clothes. Perhaps he'd changed them. But it wouldn't make any sense to change into identical clothes. I wasn't even thinking straight as I debated whether to call Stephanie or the cops or confront the guy.

I walked over to him. "Were you at the concert?"

"Yeah." He looked scared, like I'd caught him.

"Did you go by yourself?"

"Yeah, so what?"

"I'm looking for someone." I sat down.

Just then the bathroom door opened and out walked Nicole.

"Hey, Race Car," she said casually, like I'd arrived at Oakcrest. "This is my friend Michael. I know him from church, and he works here, so we can drink all the Diet Coke we want."

I looked her over. "Are you okay?"

"Yeah, I'm fine."

"We've been searching for you."

"We just came down for Diet Coke. It's hot."

"Why didn't you answer your phone?"

"It's dead. I forgot to charge it."

I called Stephanie and Eli with the good news. I didn't call Rayne, though. I figured the others would tell her.

WHEN THE THREE OF US GOT BACK TO THE PARK, Stephanie hugged Nicole and told her never to walk off like that again. With everybody surrounding her, Nicole looked pleased to be receiving so much attention. Sean told jokes to Michael and for once Nicole didn't try to stop him.

Eli came up to me. "Glad you found her. It's happened to all of us."

Stephanie lectured Nicole about telling people where she was going. Stephanie was right but I was struck by how independent Nicole had been. She'd met a friend and they'd gone to Subway for Diet Cokes. We were supposed to encourage independence, but in this case she'd been *too* independent.

Rayne kept her distance from me and I was sure she was worried about being fired, too. Stephanie thanked the police for their help and bought everybody ice-cream bars. When she handed me mine, she looked directly at me. "Be in the office first thing tomorrow morning and bring your keys. Is that clear?"

"Yes." Totally. I'd be fired for blowing my second chance.

THE NEXT MORNING I PLAYED WITH MY KEYS AS I waited outside Stephanie's office. I avoided making eye contact with Lydia, the secretary, and remembered coming to find out about the job. That seemed like ages ago, and in that time, Oakcrest had become so important. I would miss the people, the place, and the paycheck. And I hated the idea of looking for another job.

When Stephanie called me in, I was calmer than I expected. I'd blown it and was paying the price. She'd warned me, so nobody else was to blame.

"Sit down," she said, and I realized how much I'd miss her. She was a great boss. "What do you have to say for yourself?"

"It was my fault. I'm responsible."

"I told you no more mistakes, didn't I?"

"Yes, I understand why you're firing me." I placed my keys on her desk.

"Good." She paused. "I was set to fire you, but then I talked to someone who urged me to reconsider."

"What?" Was she firing me or not?

"Do you want to know whom?"

"Who? Whom?" I could never keep those straight.

"Kirsty."

"Kirsty? Why?"

"She said you'd been working hard and warned me that if I fired you and hired somebody new, that person would make the same mistake. She said after this, you'll never let Nicole out of your sight again."

I couldn't believe Kirsty was standing up for me.

"I have every right to fire you," Stephanie said, "but I'm not.

Kirsty may be right, but I need you to promise that you will pay extra attention."

"I promise. I promise." I was bursting inside as I grabbed my keys.

She held up two fingers. "Two strikes. One more and you're out."

WHEN I GOT HOME, I opened my laptop and searched for flights. I was unsure when to come back and was shocked to find that a one-way trip cost more than a round-trip ticket. That didn't make any sense, but no matter how I changed the dates, that price difference remained.

Rayne had questioned whether I'd go, and I needed to prove that I could. It was scary to think about traveling on my own, but it seemed like the best way to figure out who I was and what I wanted. I selected different dates for the return trip, but it didn't change the price much. I checked out coming back in June, but then questioned leaving Europe in the middle of summer. I'd told people I was taking a gap year. I could do it.

August 31 to August 30

The dates stared back at me from the screen. One year. Rayne was going that long and would find work to support herself even if it wasn't strictly legal. I could do that, too, especially with my Spanish. My finger hovered over the touch pad. One year. A click could have huge consequences.

I pressed down and the amount appeared. I pulled out my credit card, the one Mom had given me in case of an emergency. This was an emergency and I'd tell her before the bill came. I quickly typed in the numbers before I could change my mind. I'd just made the second-biggest decision of my life.

THE NEXT DAY AT THE EDGE, I confronted Rayne right away. "I didn't like how you hung me out with Stephanie when Nicole disappeared."

"I got scared." Rayne picked a fingernail.

"I know, but we could have handled it together."

"True," she said softly. "It wasn't fair. I'm sorry I did that."

"Good. I'm glad I still have my job." I took a long drink of iced coffee.

"Me too," Rayne said. "We need you at Oakcrest. It wouldn't be the same without you."

I pulled my flight receipt out of my pocket, unfolded it, and handed it to her.

She studied it carefully. "The same flight to Amsterdam as me? I don't believe it."

"We're not sitting together or anything like that. I know you need your space."

"Very funny." She pushed me. "You're really going to Barcelona?"

"Yeah."

She kept staring at the paper with her mouth open, and her surprise made the decision worth it. "Not many guys have the balls to travel solo."

"I know," I said. "I do."

EIGHTEENTH

AFTER MY NEAR FIRING, I kept a close eye on Nicole whenever we were out. Rayne and I got together when we could and discussed our upcoming trips. I hadn't told my parents, and it wouldn't be official until I did, but I wasn't ready. I was keeping a secret from them again, but this time, I was more in control.

For my eighteenth birthday at the end of July, Mom asked if I wanted to have a party with Uncle Ed's family. I didn't, and I suggested inviting Rayne to dinner at our house. Mom seemed surprised at my suggestion, but she agreed to it, and I could tell she was curious about her.

Mom picked up fresh veggies at the farmer's market and made two different lasagnas, one with wheat and meat and the other with rice noodles and spinach. I thought it would have been better to make something we all could eat like we had at Rayne's, but Mom ruled that out because Dad and Lansing loved meat.

I shaved and showered, and blasted body spray three different times. I was more nervous waiting for Rayne to show up and Dad to get home than I had been all summer. Rayne coming to dinner felt even bigger than my birthday. I changed my shirt twice before settling on being comfortable in shorts and a plain black T-shirt.

"You're wearing that?" Mom said when I walked into the kitchen.

"It's *my* birthday."

"What does Rayne like to drink?" She put ice into glasses.

"Juice, tea, water, anything but coffee and milk. She's not big on caffeine or dairy."

"Dairy? You didn't say anything about dairy. There's cheese in her lasagna. Is that okay?"

"Yeah, some cheese is fine."

"She's got a lot of dietary requirements for a young person." Mom raised her eyebrows. "Help put these water glasses on the table."

I set one at each plate in the dining room, and Lansing wandered in.

"What smells so good?" he asked.

"Lasagna," Mom said from the kitchen. "Rayne's coming for Cray's birthday dinner."

"Is she bringing her brother, Thunder?" Lansing laughed.

"She's smart." I gave him a shove. "Don't make stupid jokes."

The front doorbell rang and I rushed to get it. Rayne was more dressed up than I expected in tan capris, a blue top, and a silver necklace. She'd even done something to smooth down her hair so it wasn't sticking out. I thought she might show up in her bowling shoes and leopard-print top, which would have been fun.

"You look great." I stepped outside and closed the door.

"Thanks." She glanced at my shorts and T-shirt but didn't return the compliment. "It's a big house. Big yard."

"Yeah." I thought of the contrast with where she lived. I moved closer and smelled a hint of perfume. "Listen, Rayne, sometimes my brother says dumb things and my mom asks inappropriate questions and my dad gets confrontational."

"Relax," she said. "I can take care of myself and so can you."

"One more thing: don't mention Spain. I haven't told them yet."

"Don't worry. It's your day."

She was right. I opened the door and ushered her in. "Rayne's here."

WHEN DAD PULLED INTO THE GARAGE, we were all sitting in the living room drinking blueberry-pomegranate juice, a kind Mom had never gotten before. Lansing hadn't made any jokes and instead was talking with Rayne about probabilities. She knew he liked math, but I was impressed by how smoothly she'd steered the conversation to a topic he was comfortable with. Mom sat back and smiled. I think she was pleased that Rayne wasn't *more different*.

I got up to refill Rayne's glass. I didn't often invite friends over because I never knew what mood Dad would be in. My stomach churned as I waited for him to enter.

"Hi," I said quickly when he walked in.

"Happy birthday," he mumbled, and placed his iPad down.

"Thanks. Want some juice?" I held up the pitcher.

"No, I'll have a gin and tonic. Miriam, do you want to join me?"

"Sure." Mom jumped up and ushered him into the living room. "Crayton, I'd like you to meet Rayne MacCrimmon."

I set the pitcher down and watched Rayne stand up.

"Nice to meet you," Dad said.

"It's a pleasure, Dr. Franklin." Rayne looked him in the eye.

Dr. Franklin. I hadn't said anything, yet Rayne knew the magic words.

"Are those Ming vases?" She noticed Dad's treasures.

"Yes," he said. "You know your ceramics."

"A little," she said. "They're beautiful."

"Thanks. I'm glad you like them." He walked her over and pointed out favorite details.

"Let's move to the dining room," Mom said. "Everything's ready."

"Give me a second to make the drinks." Dad waved her away.

"Rayne, you'll sit here." Mom pulled out a chair. "Cray, you can be there." She pointed to my usual spot, which was now next to Rayne.

Mom set Rayne's lasagna in front of her and the big one by Lansing. She placed a bowl of green beans next to the salad and Dad sat down.

I hoped he wouldn't make us pray in front of Rayne, who didn't do that at her house, but of course he did. Rayne bowed her head and at the end I looked over and caught her eye.

"Help yourself to lasagna, Rayne," Mom said.

"Thank you." Rayne scooped some onto her plate. "This looks delicious."

"How come you don't eat wheat?" Dad looked over at Rayne.

I feared the worst, but Rayne patiently explained that she was allergic and that her grandfather was Scottish and many Celts had sensitivity to wheat since historically they'd eaten oats and barley. She wasn't defensive or embarrassed, and Dad listened and didn't argue or tell her she was wrong.

"Doesn't it make going out to eat challenging?" Mom passed Rayne the beans.

"Not really. Thai, Mexican, and Chinese are easy, and most places have vegetarian and nonwheat options now."

"Don't you miss meat?" Lansing asked.

"No, I've adjusted," Rayne said. "You can adjust to all kinds of things."

Mom, Dad, and Lansing were all checking out Rayne as she talked. They were undoubtedly surprised I was friends with someone so smart and beautiful.

Partway through dinner, we started talking about Oakcrest.

"Brent had another seizure yesterday." Rayne looked at me.

"What kind of seizure?" Mom asked.

"Tonic-clonic," I said. "He's had them his whole life." Dad looked up from his lasagna. I hadn't thought about it before, but a part of my job at Oakcrest was dealing with medical issues. Continuing the family tradition in a different way. Dad looked confused, like he was trying to process information that didn't fit.

I liked turning the tables and having him be surprised.

"THAT WAS FUN," Rayne said as we walked away from the house.

"Yeah, everybody was on their best behavior." I was impressed by how smoothly she'd handled things. I had imagined her being more confrontational with Dad. I even hoped for some of that, but instead she had engaged him in doctor talk, and he enjoyed it.

"I like your mom. She takes care of so much." Rayne paused and I guessed she was thinking about what she didn't have. "And Lansing reminds me a bit of Aaron. He's smart, but shy and pays close attention to things."

"Yeah." I hadn't thought of Lansing like that before. "I don't know why Dad had to start talking politics at the end."

"That was good," Rayne said. "Got his true feelings on social-ized medicine and the decline of America."

"But you didn't say anything back to him."

"He's not interested in my opinion, so I listened to his. You're all so scared of him."

I stopped walking and looked at her. Rayne was right. It was that simple. We all were scared of him, and she'd talked with him like she wasn't, like he was a regular person. "I know. We all try to avoid conflict with him."

"And how's that going?" Rayne asked.

"It causes a lot of conflict." I laughed. I'd always run from conflict with Dad, but by standing up to him about college, I'd cre-ated a huge conflict. And through that, I'd begun to figure some things out.

"How did you like your gifts?" Rayne asked as we walked under a canopy of trees.

"Great." Mom and Dad had gotten me the new iPhone, and Lansing had given me a cool silver case that extended the battery life. "My parents even agreed to pay my phone charges for the first year."

"That's big."

"Yeah, especially since I'll use it in Spain." I rubbed my hands on my shorts.

"Why haven't you told them yet?"

"I'm worried about how they'll react."

"Worried, or scared?"

"Both." That was one more conflict I had to face. Rayne and I crossed the street and as we did our bare arms brushed against each other and my excitement rose.

"I got you a few gifts, too," Rayne said. "I left them beside the bed at Oakcrest for you to open tonight. Happy birthday, Cray." She turned and leaned in and I wrapped my arms around her as we shared a deep, wet kiss. I remembered what had happened last time, so I didn't make any sudden moves. Instead, I slowed down, closed my eyes, and savored the sensation of my lips on hers as we explored different ways to move them together.

I relived the kiss as I hurried up the driveway to Oakcrest.

WHEN I OPENED THE DOOR, the lights went out as I stepped onto the landing.

"*Happy birthday to you, happy birthday to you,*" everybody sang loudly as Eli played guitar. Kate held a cake with eighteen candles, which provided enough light for me to see faces. I climbed the stairs, amazed that they'd done this for me.

"*Happy birthday, dear Race Car. Happy birthday to you.*" Eli strummed a dramatic conclusion and they all cheered.

"Look at the cake," Sean said.

Nicole turned on the lights and I saw the cake was in the shape of a race car.

"Awesome." I picked off a piece of frosting and tasted it.

"That's not appropriate," Nicole said.

"It's his cake," Brent said. "He can do what he wants."

"The cake's for all of us." Nicole put her hands on her hips. "We're all eating it."

"My favorite cake ever." I pulled out my new phone and took a picture.

"Eli helped us make it," Kate said.

"It says Race Car on the race car." Brent pointed.

"What are you doing up? You're never up this late."

"It's your birthday. I wanted to stay up."

"Thanks, Brent." I hugged him and then Eli, Sean, Nicole, and even Kate, who shocked me by hugging me back.

"Happy birthday, Race Car," she said.

"Thank you. This is fantastic." So we all sat down in the kitchen and ate race car cake with big scoops of chocolate ice cream.

The good feeling continued later when I went downstairs and saw Rayne's presents. They were wrapped in red and yellow paper, the colors of the Spanish flag. I started with the smallest, which was a set of black roller-ball pens. I didn't know why she'd given me them until I opened the second package, a thick blank journal. I flipped through the pages. I'd never be able to fill them. She'd also given me a DVD collection of Pedro Almodóvar movies, a plastic passport holder, and the Lonely Planet *Guide to Spain* to help me plan my trip.

When I got into bed, I paged through the guidebook. I'd fly into Barcelona, but I also wanted to go to Madrid, Seville, Córdoba, and Granada. The white beaches of the Costa del Sol, where bikini tops were optional, looked incredible. So did Pamplona with the wild running of the bulls.

I smelled Rayne's scent on the pillow. I'd persuaded her that stripping the bed after she'd slept in it four nights was bad for the environment. She had a strong green streak, so she'd agreed. The truth was I liked crawling into the same sheets she had earlier in the week.

The kiss, the cake, the presents—I'd always remember my eighteenth.

TIME TO TELL

A COUPLE OF DAYS LATER, I biked over to Jett's house. I hadn't seen him since the Fourth of July, and we hadn't talked or texted, either. That was the longest we'd ever gone with no contact.

As I approached his house, I heard the familiar beat of basketball on concrete. Jett eyed the hoop wearing a gold T-shirt that said CLUTCH.

"Hey, all set for college ball?"

"Yeah."

Jett bounced the ball, bent his knees, and released the shot. The ball swished through and I flipped it back. He was so good that most of the time the ball never even hit the rim as it splashed through the net. It was nice to be on the same court since we hadn't hooped together all summer.

"Did you hear about Teagan?" he asked.

"No, what?"

"She's been obsessing about college, and Friday she had a breakdown. She's in St. Mary's."

"Oh no, have you seen her?"

"No, she's not seeing friends, not even Nora, just family."

"I'm really sorry." I thought back to graduation and that gas station kiss and how she'd said the college application process was crazy. I also remembered her brother from the movie theater and thought about how scary it must be to see his sister that way.

I rebounded and passed the ball to Jett like we'd done hundreds of times. Neither one of us knew what to say.

Finally Jett broke the silence. "I've got orientation at Duluth in two weeks."

I nodded but was still thinking about Teagan. She'd wanted me to call and I hadn't. That wouldn't have prevented this, but it wouldn't have hurt.

"Nora starts at Stanford next month." He wiped his face with his sleeve. "We're not going to see each other until Thanksgiving." The ball hit the rim and bounced off and I tapped it in.

"That's a long time."

Jett backed off the line and looked like he was considering something. "We had a long talk last night. Nora says we should break up so we can meet new people at college. She thinks it's best to have a fresh start."

"What do you think?"

"We don't need to do that. Why can't we just wait and see what happens?" He missed another shot and shook out his hands.

"Yeah." I turned around and banked the ball off the board. I knew how much he was into her. I debated telling him that it would be okay and he'd meet loads of new girls, but that didn't seem like what he needed to hear. "Sorry."

I remembered what Rayne had said about Nora using people.

She needed a precollege summer boyfriend, and that was Jett. She'd gotten what she'd wanted and he hadn't realized that was all it was.

I continued to rebound. Jett and Nora, the two who had warned me about Rayne. I should have warned him about her.

"You can come up to visit." The ball flicked through the net as he found his stroke.

"I'd like to, but I'm going to Europe."

"Where?"

"Spain. I leave the end of August." I bounced the ball to him. "We can Skype. I want to hear how college goes."

"You're traveling by yourself?"

"Yeah, I'm flying over with Rayne, but she's going to Scotland while I go to Spain."

"Wow," Jett said. "Come up when you're back."

"I won't be back for a year."

"Seriously?" Jett held the ball under his arm.

"Yeah, I'm traveling for my gap year." As I said it, I wasn't bragging. I was still convincing myself that I could.

THE TIME HAD COME TO FINALLY TELL MOM AND DAD. I picked a dinner and waited until Dad finished his steak and was in a good mood after a couple of drinks.

"I've made a plan for my gap year," I announced.

"Your what?" Lansing asked.

"What I'm doing this school year."

"What's your plan?" Mom wiped her mouth with her napkin.

"I'm going to Spain."

"Spain?" Mom looked as if I'd said Mars.

"You're going to Spain?" Lansing looked wide-eyed.

"I thought I told you not to go," Dad said.

"That was Scotland. I'm not going there. I'm going to Spain. It's my decision." I held my thigh to stop my heel tapping. Dad was being extreme, even for him, about Europe. Then it hit me. That was where his brother Stevie, the one he didn't talk about, had died.

"How will you pay for this trip?" He shook the ice in his glass.

"I've got money in savings for the ticket and the first few months and I'll pick up work over there. I'll teach English or tutor or translate."

"Are you going with Rayne?" Mom asked.

"No, she's going to Scotland. I'm going solo."

"Are you sure?" Mom said. "I don't know—"

"Let him go, Miriam," Dad cut her off. "He'll find out how hard it is to be out on his own."

"You're really going." Lansing leaned in.

"Don't you get any ideas from this, Lansing," Dad warned.

"He's already got his own ideas." I looked over at my brother. "You can't control ideas."

"That's enough." Dad pointed at me. "You're not the parent here. You can't even take care of yourself."

"How long will you be gone?" Mom asked.

"A year." I tried to sound confident.

"A year? A *year*? That's way too long." Her voice started to shake. "You won't be here for Thanksgiving and Christmas? Our family's always been together for the holidays. You have to be here."

"Don't worry," Dad announced. "He'll be back by then."

I shook my head. Mom didn't want me to go. Dad didn't think I'd stay. I had to do this for myself.

"When do you leave?" Mom clenched her hands.

"August thirty-first."

"That's next month," she said.

"You've got no idea what you're doing." Dad stuck out his lower lip in a frown.

That wasn't true and I guessed he probably knew that.

"You should have accepted our college offer," Dad said. "That would have made everything easier."

Easy wasn't the best reason to do things, but I wasn't going to argue with him. Besides, if he wasn't backing down on college, then neither was I. We were like two grizzly bears locked in a struggle. Maybe Mom was right. I was like him sometimes. I could dig in and refuse to give ground when I thought I was right, just like him. I was his son, after all. But by traveling, I was making damn sure I was different, too.

I sat back in my chair and looked over at Lansing, who smiled at me, like he couldn't believe what had just happened. Rayne had said we were all afraid of Dad. I tried not to show it. "I'm going to Spain. I'll pay my rent for August and then go."

"Mark my words." Dad tapped the table. "You'll be back in a month."

I got up and took my plate and silverware to the dishwasher. I wasn't coming back early. I was way too stubborn—too much like him—to do that.

LATER, AS I APPROACHED OAKCREST, I was shocked to see a police car's flashing lights in the driveway. Different disaster scenarios ran through my mind. Had Brent had another seizure? Had Nicole cut herself again? Was it even worse?

Nobody was in the car, so I ran up the steps and burst in. Brent, Eli, and a cop turned to look at me.

"This is Cray. He works here," Eli said.

"What's going on?" I sat down with them.

"He said I was drunk." Brent pointed at the cop. "He threw me down and broke my glasses and put handcuffs on me and made me get in the back of the police car. I don't drink. I can't because of my meds."

"He was staggering along the side of the road." The young cop smoothed his mustache. "When I talked to him, he argued with me even when I threatened him with arrest."

"This is all a misunderstanding." Eli waved his hand.

"I was coming back from Dairy Queen, minding my own business," Brent said.

"Brent is on medication for seizures," Eli explained. "An unsteady gait is one of the side effects."

"I can't help it." Brent held out his hand and it shook.

"It would be good for him to go with a friend or have one of you drive him next time," the cop suggested.

"Brent goes lots of places on his own," I spoke up. "He wants to be as independent as possible. That's our goal for everybody here."

"All the neighbors and most of the police officers know Brent," Eli added.

The cop looked down and didn't say anything for a while. "I'm new. I see I made a mistake." He turned toward Brent. "I'm sorry."

"That's okay."

I'd never heard a cop apologize before.

"I'm Jason." The cop walked over and shook hands with Brent.

"If you ever need help or need a ride in an emergency, give me a call." He presented Brent with a card.

"Okay," Brent said. "I will."

AS SOON AS JASON LEFT, Kate, Sean, and Nicole came out of their rooms and started asking questions. Eli said good-bye since it was after ten and he was meeting friends. Brent described in detail how he was walking back to the house eating his ice-cream cone when the cop pulled up and accused him of being drunk.

"He didn't listen to anything," Brent said. "And my dipped cone got knocked to the ground. I'm going to Dairy Queen tomorrow to tell the manager and see if she'll give me another one."

"Good idea," I said. "We'll get your glasses fixed, and Jason did apologize."

"And now he's going to give me free rides in the police car to the mall or anywhere I want to go." Brent grinned.

"No fair," Sean protested.

"Can I ride with you?" Nicole asked.

"No, just me." Brent shook his head.

"I think that was only in case of an emergency," I said.

"Hey, Race Car, what do you call a bear with no shoes?" Sean asked.

"A bear? I don't know."

"What about you, Kate?" Sean said. "A bear with no shoes."

"I don't know."

"Barefoot." Sean roared with laughter. "Barefoot!"

I started laughing and it felt like a release. Everybody else was laughing with him. Everybody except Nicole. "Sean, it's too late for jokes."

"It's never too late for jokes." He started telling another one about a chicken and a hamster.

I looked around at the people in the room. I had plenty in common with Brent, Nicole, Sean, and Kate. They were trying to live as independently as possible.

So was I.

UNINVITED

EARLY ONE MORNING ON MY SECOND-TO-LAST WEEK
of work, I woke up to Chimney meowing near my head. I checked
the time and saw it was just after five, way too early for his breakfast. I brushed him away and rolled over to go back to sleep. But he
wouldn't leave, so I pushed him off the bed.

He meowed from the floor and jumped back up by my pillow.

"What's the matter?"

"Meeeeeeooooooowww."

I sat up and listened but didn't hear anything unusual. I lay
back down but couldn't fall asleep with Chimney making noise.

I got up, put on my jeans, and went upstairs. I looked out the
front window into the dark and noticed nothing.

Chimney meowed from the hall so I went down to check.

At Brent's door, I heard snoring. Same thing at Sean's. At Nicole's, it was silent, but then the bed squeaked as she shifted position. At Kate's, though, I heard nothing. I remembered Stephanie's

warning about going into people's rooms uninvited. Kate was probably sleeping peacefully and I was imagining things.

Chimney popped into Kate's room through the cat door and I started to go back downstairs, but a gut feeling tugged at me. I was afraid that if I didn't check I'd regret it. I knocked on the door.

No answer.

"Kate."

No answer. Just Chimney meowing.

I gently turned the handle and peeked in. Kate wasn't in her bed! I opened the door wide and saw her lying spread out on her back on the floor with Chimney circling her. I turned on the light, and saw Kate's chest wasn't rising or falling.

"Kate!" I grabbed her wrist, which felt cool. I checked her neck but didn't find a pulse. "Kate!" I shook her shoulder, but she didn't wake up.

I reached for my phone, but it wasn't in my pocket. I rushed out, tripped in the hallway, scrambled up, jumped down the stairs, raced to the table by the bed, and grabbed it. I quickly punched in 911. "I need an ambulance for 709 Oakcrest Court. Fast. Kate's not breathing."

"An ambulance is on the way," the dispatcher said. "My name is Gloria. Do you know how to do CPR?"

"I had a class in school, but I don't remember much."

"I'll guide you through it. Can you put me on speakerphone?"

"Yeah." I turned that on as I hurried to Kate's room. I shook her again, hoping for a miracle.

"Is the patient on her back?" Gloria asked.

"Yes."

"Put one hand on top of the other and spread your fingers,"

Gloria said. "Press down solidly on the middle of the chest exactly between the nipples with the heel of your hand."

I positioned myself over Kate and did what she said as Chimney watched from the bed.

"Push hard and steady," Gloria said. "The chest should go down two inches and then come all the way back up. Then press down again."

I pressed hard but grew concerned. "What if I hurt her?"

"Don't worry about that," Gloria said. "You're trying to save her life. One hundred beats per minute. Push...push...push...push."

"Don't...die...Kate. Don't...die...Kate," I repeated to myself as I pressed down.

"Do you know the Bee Gees song 'Stayin' Alive'?" Gloria asked.

"No. What? Why?"

"That's the rhythm to follow." Gloria sang in a high voice and added extra emphasis on the beats as I kept pressing on Kate's chest.

"What about the breath?" I couldn't imagine putting my mouth on Kate's and breathing in.

"The compressions are sufficient," Gloria said. She put even more energy into the chorus of "Stayin' Alive."

All of a sudden, I remembered the front door was locked. "Brent, Sean, Nicole!" I hollered as loud as I could, and Chimney jumped off the bed and ran out.

"What's going on?" Gloria shouted.

"Sorry." I explained and yelled for them again as I kept up the steady rhythm of compressions.

Nicole emerged first in her Justin Bieber robe and pajamas, and Brent staggered in looking still asleep.

"Nicole, unlock the front door for the paramedics. Brent, call

Stephanie and tell her Kate's unconscious and an ambulance is on the way." I kept pressing down. "Come on, Kate. Come on, Kate," I pleaded as seconds ticked into minutes.

"Don't let up. Keep pressing hard. One hundred beats a minute," Gloria said quickly, then resumed singing.

"Stayin' Alive," that's exactly what we wanted for Kate. I pressed away to Gloria's beat.

Finally I heard the paramedics at the door.

"Up here," I shouted as Nicole introduced herself to them.

A man and a woman burst into Kate's room carrying their equipment and ushering me out. I went to check on Brent and Nicole in the living room. Brent was pulling his hair and Nicole was pacing.

"What's going to happen to Kate?" Brent asked.

"I don't know." I heard the defibrillator trying to shock her heart back to beating.

"Is she dead?" Nicole continued pacing.

"No, no. I don't know." I sat down and rubbed my eyes.

"Should we wake Sean to tell him?" Nicole asked.

"No, let him sleep until we know more." Their questions were making me nervous, so I motioned for them to sit down. My heel was tapping a million miles an hour as I heard the paramedics discuss getting Kate onto a stretcher.

They came out with her strapped on and not moving.

"Is she going to be okay?" I jumped down the steps to hold the door open for them.

"We don't know," the woman said.

Nicole and Brent came to the door and we watched them slide the stretcher in the back of the ambulance. It sped off with the lights flashing but without the siren on. I didn't like that. I wanted the siren blaring to let everybody know that Kate was in trouble.

When we went back inside, there was no way I could go back to sleep, so I made coffee, and Brent and Nicole said they wanted some, too. The three of us sat together clutching hot mugs as the first signs of light edged out the darkness. I thought about Kate and how uncomfortable she'd made me feel when I started, with her anxiety and arm biting. I'd grown to like her and she liked me, too. I couldn't handle the idea of someone dying while I was in charge. I knew that was selfish, but it was real. I replayed everything and wished I'd gotten to her sooner and had my phone with me when I did.

I thought about how initially I'd believed the job was getting paid to sleep. It had turned out to be way more than that—life and death.

The phone rang and I jumped up. Stephanie had found out Kate's hospital and was on her way there. "I'll call when I have news. Please reassure everybody."

I hung up and didn't know how to reassure anybody. Brent and Nicole looked at me and I told them Stephanie was going to the hospital.

"I'll wake Sean up so he knows," Nicole announced.

"I'm going to find Chimney." Brent got up.

"That's good." I heard someone at the door and wondered who it could be so early. I went over to the stairs and was grateful to see Rayne.

"I heard from Stephanie." She wrapped me in a hug. I hung on tightly like she was a lifesaver and the world was an ocean. "I'm so sorry," she whispered.

And then the tears came, first softly, and then harder. I cried more than I had in a long time, as I held on to Rayne, who was crying, too.

"Stop it, you babies." Brent petted Chimney. "Stephanie will know what to do."

I wiped my tears. I was supposed to be reassuring him and instead he was reassuring me. "I'm sorry."

"For what?" Rayne asked.

"For crying."

"That's fine." She handed me a tissue.

WE ALL GATHERED IN THE LIVING ROOM, including Sean, who was upset we hadn't woken him earlier.

"That was my fault." I tapped my chest.

"That's okay, Race Car," Nicole said.

"No, it's not." Sean shook his head.

The house phone rang and I rose to get it.

"I've got bad news," Stephanie said, her voice trembling. "Kate suffered a massive heart attack. The doctors couldn't save her."

I stared out the window at the twisted branches of the oak tree and thought about how one minute a person could be alive and then all of a sudden dead.

"The paramedics were impressed by what you did, Cray," she said. "But you couldn't have saved her."

I appreciated her trying to make me feel better, but that seemed insignificant. "I'm sorry, Stephanie."

"I'm sorry for all of us. We're going to miss her terribly. Can you tell people?"

"Yeah. Rayne is here, too."

"Good."

I hung up and turned to see everybody watching me. I knew I had to be as clear as possible. "Kate died. She suffered a heart attack."

I walked toward Rayne and she stood to give me a hug. Nicole got up and wrapped her arms around us. Then Sean and Brent did, too. The five of us stood together and tears flowed.

For the second time that morning I was crying, and it felt like the appropriate response—the age-appropriate response for all of us.

THE NEXT FEW DAYS WERE A BLUR AS I STRUGGLED TO catch up to what had happened. Kate's things got cleaned out and painters came to put a fresh coat of white on the walls. I walked around in a daze and kept Kate's door closed when I worked. I hoped she would open it and walk out, and everything would go back to normal.

The day of the funeral was a relief in a way because everybody focused on the same thing. Grace Lutheran Church was packed with Kate's friends, family, coworkers, and people from the other CSS houses. I sat between Rayne and Nicole in a pew of Oakcrest people. Sean tightened his tie and Brent looked down. Nicole dabbed her eyes with a tissue and I reached to hold her hand. I grabbed Rayne's on the other side and she reached out to Brent. Pretty soon everybody from Oakcrest, including Eli, Stephanie, Kirsty, and Darla, were holding hands together.

The pastor described how Kate had been anxious and suspicious when he first met her. "But once she liked you, there was nobody more loyal."

I looked around the church. It seemed a number of people had gone through the same thing I had with Kate. The pastor was right. She didn't accept people easily, but once she did, she accepted them totally.

Kate's sister, who looked a lot like her, talked about how close the two of them became after their mother died. She said she spoke on the phone with Kate every day and, depending on what was going on, sometimes multiple times a day. "Her voice is so clear in my head that my daily conversations with her will continue."

Kate's father also got up. He was an old man with a white beard who walked with a cane, but he spoke strongly. He thanked everybody at Oakcrest, including somebody he said Kate called Race Car. Everybody laughed, and I was surprised to be singled out. "Thank you for everything you did to provide Kate with such a full life. We could never have done it without you."

I gave Rayne's hand a squeeze and she smiled softly through her tears.

BEGINNING

LATER THAT WEEK, Rayne and I walked among the cemetery gravestones. Acorns fell on the path, and the earlier dark hinted of fall. A place that had once seemed scary now felt familiar. I thought about being with everybody at the funeral. "I'm going to miss Oakcrest when I leave."

"Me too." Rayne picked up a plastic bag that had wrapped around a gravestone and shoved it in her pocket. "You've really connected with people there. Stephanie would hire you back in a second."

I'd been so focused on leaving that I hadn't thought about coming back. It was reassuring to know I had a place there.

Rayne turned to me. "Getting excited about Barcelona?"

"Yeah, I've got a youth hostel lined up for a week, and there are so many other places I want to see. That guide you gave me is great. I'm going to Madrid, where many of those Almodóvar films are set, and then to the Alhambra in Granada and the Mezquita, the giant cathedral that used to be a mosque, in Córdoba. Southern Spain is very close to Morocco, so I can take a ferry to Tangier and be in North Africa, on a different continent, and go to Casablanca and Marrakesh."

"How are your parents handling it?" Rayne asked.

"Dad's not saying I'll be home in a month anymore. He's switched it to the end of the year, which is progress. Mom shocked me by giving me back all the rent money. She didn't think I should have been paying it in the first place and told me not to tell Dad but to use it for my trip. And Lansing came up with the idea of them meeting me in Spain for Christmas. Mom said if I was there then, she wanted to do it, and Dad didn't rule it out."

"Wow."

"Yeah, the clearer I've been about going, the fewer arguments I've had with them and the more they've accepted it. In a strange way, it seems Dad even wants me to go. He keeps saying it will show me how great college is, but I also think he wants me out of the house. He worries I'm a bad influence on Lansing, but I think he's jealous."

"Why?"

"He's always been into art and stuff from around the world but he's hardly traveled. I bet he would have liked to but got scared after his brother died." I told Rayne the story of Stevie as we walked, and she listened closely. "I think Dad wishes he'd done what I'm doing."

"That's interesting," Rayne said.

"Dad knows I'm not going to St. Luke's and isn't sure what to do. I hope being independent and on my own for a year will change how he sees me."

"That's huge." Rayne gave me a fist bump.

"Yeah." We walked down the hill to the new section of the cemetery, and an owl hooted a lonely call. We stopped in front of a freshly dug grave with dirt mounded on top. I bent down to examine the temporary marker. I couldn't read it in the dark so I took out my phone and tapped the flashlight on.

"Is it?" Rayne asked.

I nodded as the two of us stood over Kate's grave. I said a silent prayer for her and for us.

"Safe crossing, Kate," Rayne said.

I crouched down and picked up a clump of dirt. Life could end so quickly: Kate, Stevie, me that time I almost got hit by the car.

Rayne squatted down beside me and reached for my other hand. "Do you know the Mary Oliver poem 'The Summer Day'?"

"No."

"It's one I love. She starts by describing how amazing a grasshopper is. Then she goes into how we're all going to die and closes with a question: 'What is it you plan to do with your one wild and precious life?'"

I felt the cool dirt in one hand and the warmth of Rayne in the other. I liked that line and finally knew. I was going to live my one wild and precious life. I couldn't live it for someone else. Not Mom. Not Dad. Not even Rayne. I needed to live it for myself.

"Farewell, dear Kate." Rayne let go and stood up.

I crumbled the dirt and it fell on the grave.

"I'm glad we came here," Rayne said as we walked up the hill.

"Me too."

"I've been thinking," she said when we were back in the older part of the cemetery. "If we're on the same flight to Amsterdam, it would be silly to sit apart."

"I agree." I went over to the statue of Zoran and rubbed his nose for good luck.

"Window or aisle?"

"What?"

"There are two seats on the side in that plane. Which do you want?"

"Window, definitely. I want to see."

"I wasn't sure you'd go," Rayne said.

"I'm going." I sat down on Mr. Driggs's grave and leaned back. I tried to sound low-key even though I was bursting inside. I was flying overnight to Europe with Rayne MacCrimmon beside me. When we got to Amsterdam, she'd go to Scotland and I'd go to Spain, but who knew what would happen after that? A year was a long time, and those places weren't that far apart. We could meet up someplace fun like London or Paris or Casablanca or Marrakesh.

I thought back to the first time I'd met Rayne at the Edge and how much had changed. "Sing that song again, the one your grandpa used to sing."

Speed, bonnie boat, like a bird on the wing,
Onward! the sailors cry;
Carry the lord that's born to be King
Over the sea to Skye.

Her voice was strong and clear.

Loud the winds howl, loud the waves roar,
Thunderclaps rend the air;
Baffled, our foes stand by the shore,
Follow they will not dare.

I joined in on the chorus and we sang together sitting side by side among the gravestones with Kate's newly dug plot down the hill.

Speed, bonnie boat, like a bird on the wing,
Onward! the sailors cry;
Carry the lord that's born to be King
Over the sea to Skye.

Onward! I was going over the sea to explore a world that was so much bigger than Clairemont, bigger than college, bigger than what I could imagine. I wasn't ruining my future like Dad had warned. I was living my gap life, my wild and precious life.

"I can't believe everything that's happened this summer." I peered into Rayne's bright eyes.

"You should write it down," she said.

So I did.

From the beginning.

ACKNOWLEDGMENTS

For ten years, I worked in group homes, residential facilities, and community houses and the experience changed my life. I am grateful for all that I learned from the people at Carlson Group Home and First Avenue of Hammer Residences and Hill House at Mount Olivet Rolling Acres. Thanks to Kim Becker, Terry Benson, Steve Bristol, Greg Burns, Bob Clough, Mary Coleman, Mary Ruder Daniels, Jim Davis, Gary Gore, Livia Gunther, Liz Koltes, Art Lehmann, Shelly Marano, Noel Pauly, Chip Pearson, Debbie Pearson, Don Rudd, Ken Sprute, Denny Spurling, Lynn Steinman, Jim Stone, Missy Swanson, Steve Tschimperle, Janet Tuckner, Lynn Vertnik, Virginia Volkenant, Steve Wilmes, and Wendy Zahn. Special thanks to the best boss one could have: Lisbeth Vest Armstrong.

Thanks to David LaRochelle, Janet Lawson, Jody Peterson Lodge, Cindy Rogers, and Mike Wohnoutka for making this so much better. Thanks to Eibhlin Caimbeul, Maddie Coy-Bjork, Joe McCrae, and Geoff Herbach for excellent ideas and suggestions.

My deep appreciation goes to everybody at the Anderson Center in Red Wing, Minnesota, for the gift of time and space.

Andrea Cascardi offered essential encouragement and guidance in shaping this story, and Liz Szabla is an absolute gift as an editor. Thank you, too, to Anna Booth for a great cover and to all my friends at Feiwel and Friends.

Onward!